Karen Parnell trained in health and safety and local government. Karen has a love of cats (she has three) and theatre as well as an interest in politics, cinema and ballet. She lives in Stratford-Upon-Avon.

Karen D. Parnell

LONDON'S SAVIOUR WITCH

AUSTIN MACAULEY
PUBLISHERS LTD.

A CIP catalogue record for this title is available from the British Library.

ISBN 9781786128461 (Paperback)
ISBN 9781786128478 (Hardback)
ISBN 9781786128485 (E-Book)
www.austinmacauley.com

First Published (2016)
Austin Macauley Publishers Ltd.
25 Canada Square
Canary Wharf
London
E14 5LQ

Prologue

Nature has always had more force than education.

Voltaire.

    Morgan Martin had always rather relished being the slightly odd and weird person that she was, she considered it to be her individuality and she had many qualities which others didn't seem to possess.

All she really wanted was to retire or perhaps to be the arts correspondent for her local newspaper and live a quiet life with her cat but due to what she could see and certainly didn't necessarily always want to see she had become embroiled in three people's lives in London when she hadn't even met them as she lived nowhere near them

    She was quite happy to help animals if required but had no burning desire to help these people who she would much rather stopped invading her personal space.

    Still, maybe if she could sort out whatever they wanted she could go back to the slovenly uninterrupted existence with her cat which was the only real ambition she held.

Chapter One

Night Flying

John Lennon once said that when you look into the sky you think of it as far away, but if you follow it down with your eyes you're standing in sky; Morgan Martin had often thought this to be a good mantra.

Tonight, she found herself looking down on her crumpled unmade bed with her beautiful black furry cat Mally snuggled up fast asleep with his head resting comfortably on the turned back purple velvet duvet.

She was mildly perturbed at being in this position as she had been dreaming about the beautiful ballet dancer Denis Rodkin as Prince Siegfried in a production of Swan Lake which she had seen the previous week, which was magical and now she was dangling just underneath the ceiling.

It might appear somewhat odd to most people to be floating just under the ceiling and having to decide if you are dreaming the scene before you, or if you are in fact awake and floating, but Morgan had long since worked out that if she was looking down on her own sleeping form under the duvet she was dreaming, but if like now there was only Mally in the bed she was most definitely really floating and there would doubtless be some matter she didn't yet know about which would require her input.

Morgan had always been somewhat different from most people and there were some qualities which she possessed of which she was unaware of anybody else who did.

The first time she had found herself floating like this was shortly after her mother's death nearly a year ago and to say she found it more than a little disconcerting would be an understatement.

She had not known what was happening and had flayed her arms around in a panic not knowing how to get back down. Mally had sat bolt upright on the bed looking at her as if she had gone mad. Eventually, she had worked out that if she looked at where she wanted to go and pointed her fingers at her chosen destination that would be where she ended up, but on that first night she just lunged for the duvet and pulled it back over her while shaking and wondering what on earth had just happened.

Since then she had realized there was a reason for her having these abilities and she calmly looked at the multi-coloured rug by her bed and pointed her fingers in that direction. She gracefully landed on the spot she had focused on.

Morgan was grateful she hadn't had too much to drink the previous evening, just a nightcap of whisky and milk in fact, because alcohol really made her question what on Earth was happening to her at times like this and it made her properly question why.

She also wondered occasionally what the police would do if they found her floating under the influence of alcohol in the early hours of a morning and she smiled to herself at the thought of how she could possibly explain that one away – "Honest Officer, I was just floating along minding my own business and not hurting anyone."

Looking at the illuminated display on the digital alarm clock through the darkness she could see that it was 2.00am. Morgan really hoped whatever she had been woken up for wouldn't take too long as she had to get some sleep and be in work at 10.00am the same morning.

The moonlight shone onto the small bronze statue of the Egyptian cat goddess Bastet which took pride of place on the bedroom windowsill and she looked at it admiringly.

She hastily dressed in her burgundy cords, a red fluffy jumper, and her fringed red cowboy boots and gave Mally a stroke, and a kiss, and ruffled his head in farewell.

After picking up her house keys from the glass bowl in front of the mirror in her hall she put a brush through her long red hair, but she was also noting the scenes in the background of her image in the mirror as she did so.

As she brushed the thick red hair which grew in all directions and made herself look presentable she could see a most beautiful pure white kitten sitting in front of a red door which had a number nine embossed in brass on it. To the top right of her reflection and to the bottom left of the mirror were two young boys playing marbles in a playground together and laughing happily as they did so, one had blonde hair and the other dark brown, and both had pudding bowl haircuts. As yet she had no idea what these images meant, but as she closed the front door behind her and went out into the cool, dark night she knew it would become evident in the near future.

That was another reason she knew that she was awake, the weather. She had never knowingly felt the cold while she was asleep. The other giveaway was that she often wanted a drink of pop, or some chocolate, or a cheese and onion sandwich when she woke up, again something she had never knowingly craved in her sleep.

Morgan had often dreamed of things which seemingly had no significance until the events that followed were connected to them in some way. It used to be dreaming of a person she didn't know and then finding that she would meet that person in the ensuing days, or sometimes dreaming of an event, such as in a film plot, and then finding that scene replayed in a film she had never seen before which she watched shortly afterwards; that was particularly annoying as she would realize she knew the ending to the film halfway through.

There was nobody around in the quiet road where she lived as she pointed skywards and floated gently upwards and hovered over the top of the lamp post across the road from her bedroom window where she paused, and waved a loving farewell to Mally who now had one eye open while watching her from their bed in the warm.

Chris and Daniel were having a few pints and a catch up as they hadn't been on a proper night out together since Daniel had got made redundant from the insurance company they had both worked at. It was an awkward subject between them and Chris was making a point of getting the drinks in as he felt guilty about it. Daniel in turn felt bad that he couldn't afford to pay his way especially when Chris had paid for them both to get into Cordelia's, the nightclub in Stratford.

They had been to three pubs before that in the evening and had played a few games of pool in the Old Bull as they laughed and joked about the many situations and scrapes they had been involved in together over the years. Chris had booked the next day off from work as holiday so they could make a proper night of it.

By now they were just beyond tipsy and Daniel insisted on getting the first round in at the club. He instantly regretted his pride when the barmaid told him the exorbitant price, but she was a pretty girl with a winning smile in a low cut top so that absorbed the blow slightly.

The club was quiet and what appeared to be the manager whispered a few words in the pretty barmaid's ear after which she picked up her handbag and opened the hatch in the bar, "See you tomorrow then if you're sure Mike. Oh, and I'll have that glass of Merlot the guy bought me earlier when you've got a minute please."

"Sure Cheryl, no point in us both working when there are less than ten punters in the club." And, placing the glass of wine on the bar before her he smiled at her, "Enjoy yourself girl."

Feeling rather brave because of the alcohol Daniel made a beeline for the girl, "You're more than welcome to join me and my mate if you'd like to," and he gestured across at the table which Chris was sitting at. "Why not," smiled Cheryl and she teetered across to the table in her patent leather high heels somewhat uncertainly.

Cheryl thought Chis and Daniel to be pleasant looking young men and was quite happy to join them for a chat and maybe a free drink or two, but she was resolutely single and certainly not in the market for a boyfriend or even a date for that matter.

The three of them chatted pleasantly and Chris bought Cheryl another couple of large glasses of wine when he got the next two rounds in for her and Daniel.

It was starting to annoy Daniel by now. The girl he had brought over to the table was concentrating her energy and conversation on Chris because he kept buying her drinks.

He knew this wasn't really about the girl or his mate: It was about the elephant in the room which was his lack of employment, current limited prospects, and finances and alcohol was certainly not improving his mind-set one bit.

Cheryl finished her last glass of wine with undue haste because she could pick up on some tension in the air between the men and she went to the cloakroom to collect her far from sexy, but very warm and comfy black duvet coat. She popped back to the table to say farewell to Chris and Daniel and gave them both a peck on the cheek while bidding them farewell before taking herself off on the short walk back to her flat where she was looking forward to reading the next chapter of her detective novel.

"I don't know about you mate but I'm ready to call it a night," said Chris, finishing off the last inch of his pint of lager, "Shall I book us a taxi?"

Still begrudging his friends generosity, Daniel said pointedly, "No mate, you've spent quite enough money tonight, let's walk."

The two men lived only ten minutes apart and so embarked on the walk home together in near silence. "OK, what's up?" asked Chris eventually. "Nothing," said Daniel, looking at the pavement as he continued walking with a slight stagger while sulking. The colder air had made him realize he had drunk at least two pints too many.

They continued for another five minutes in silence before the now stewing Daniel volunteered, "I brought that girl over to our table and you kept trying to buy her with wine!" he spluttered.

"I didn't fancy her one bit. Just being polite," shrugged Chris. "When you sober up you'll think this conversation absurd mate." But that was like a red rag to a bull, and in Daniel's sozzled state he pushed his friend none to gently on the shoulder into the holly bush by the pavement. Chris turned around awkwardly in the bush and looked at the hurt and angry expression on Daniel's face, "Look mate, I only want to give you a hand, cheer you up a bit, I know you're having a rough time of it at the moment."

Morgan had headed straight to the river since she didn't know where she was supposed to be heading to. She gravitated to water anyway and loved floating above it looking down at its darkness and serenity. Tonight the river was rippling gently beneath her and shimmering under the moonlight, it was quite beautiful.

She then floated at speed, just the once up the length of the river, which was exhilarating if very cooling and then floated back down its length at a far more sedate pace watching the roosting birds by the water's edge from a height of about ten feet above the water when she thought she had better do a lap or two of the housing estates.

It wasn't long before she heard the sound of two men arguing and she pointed her fingers at a large oak tree where she floated down gently on to a large branch to

16

watch the two men beneath her. One of which was struggling to get out of a bush.

One had dark hair and the other fair hair just like the two boys she had seen in her mirror. She instinctively knew these were the same people but more than a little bit older and seemingly drunker. She closed her eyes and concentrated on the image she had seen of these men as young boys.

She then opened her eyes and stared directly at the two men willing them to see their younger selves too.

A short silence followed and then Daniel put out his hand to help his friend out of the bush, "I'm so sorry mate. I've been a monumental Prat. Do you know I just looked at you in that bush and saw an image of us laughing and playing marbles together years ago?"

"Odd," said Chris taking his friend's hand as they fell into a bear hug while laughing together, "I just saw that image too, in a playground somewhere donkeys years ago."

Morgan watched as they clumsily walked up the road together arm in arm while still laughing as they wandered off into the distance zig-zagging slightly as they did so.

All was silent now except for a faint meowing sound. Looking down from the branch she had perched on she looked into the beautiful bright blue eyes of a pure white cat who was eyeing her quizzically.

Gently pointing at a spot adjacent to the cat she gently floated down and bent down to give the cat a stoke on the head and a tickle behind the ears.

"I think you've strayed a little too far from home, gorgeous one, haven't you?" The cat purred and rubbed against her legs and appeared to meow her agreement.

Looking at the disc on her collar Morgan said gently, "Well I'd better get you home then Coppelia, somebody will be worried where you have got to at this late hour."

Indeed they were. Maggie-Ann Jones was getting up at hourly intervals and calling Coppelia's name at a whisper while walking up and down the road searching with a torch in her paisley pyjamas and bright pink fleece dressing gown. She was worried sick, Coppelia was the love of her life and she had never stayed out this late before.

Gently picking the now purring Coppelia up Morgan closed her eyes and concentrated on the image of her she had seen in her mirror, she again saw the red door with the number nine embossed in brass on it, but this time she tried to see the surrounding area to this and as she concentrated she saw a huge amount of poplar trees and a street sign a little further down from them which spelled out Avenue Road. This was not far from where Morgan and Mally lived, so hugging Coppelia close to her with her left arm she pointed skywards and was gently floating over the street lamps while quietly reassuring Coppelia not to worry and that she would be home soon.

Morgan had no powers at all to ensure that she could not to be seen by anybody, it was simply that she only flew at night while being mindful of how people may react to seeing a low flying woman, and anyway nobody ever seemed to look up at the sky.

Coppelia was enjoying the bird's eye view of her local area and watched agog as the tree tops gently swayed beneath her. It was only a short journey to Avenue Road and Morgan floated gently down by the street sign and gave Coppelia a hug and a kiss before gently placing her down on the pavement. A couple of hundred yards up the road a woman in a bright pink dressing gown and holding a torch was pacing up and down the pavement. Coppelia meowed as her name was whispered quietly in the darkness and Morgan asked her, "Is that your mum then?" Appearing to meow her agreement Coppelia nuzzled Morgan's ankles affectionately before trotting up the road to rejoin Maggie-Ann. She looked back once as if to say farewell and thanks and Morgan winked at her from behind the tree which she had taken cover behind.

Another meow and Maggie-Ann turned around to see her beloved cat. She scooped her into her arms and kissed her white head while saying, "I've been so worried about you, where have you been angel?" Coppelia nuzzled into her face which now had tears of relief running down it and into Coppelia's fur and Morgan watched as they both went behind their front door with Maggie-Ann closing it behind them with a huge smile on her face as she put Coppelia down on the doormat, who gently trotted into the house behind her mum.

Feeling she had done what was required of her for this evening and with a sense of pride at the results of her input Morgan gently floated back home. She let herself in and proceeded straight upstairs where she put her pyjamas back on and got back into bed trying not to wake up Mally, who was happily snoring on the other side of the duvet.

The excursion had only taken around half an hour so she still had plenty of time to get some sleep in before she would have to go to work at the Stratford Chronicle.

Rolling over and pulling the duvet over herself she put her arm around Mally, who rewarded her with a contented purr as they went back to sleep cuddled up together.

As she nodded back off to sleep a lovely image of Glastonbury Tor with the sun rising behind it came into her mind and she saw a much younger version of herself staring at it in awe with her parents standing smiling beside her.

Chapter Two

Weird Beginnings

Morgan was an only child and she had always been more comfortable on her own than when she was around other people. At school she had always been singled out as being a bit different as she was very shy and didn't interact with the other children. This had ensured she was bullied and called names, nothing too serious but she had decided at a very young age that she much preferred the company of animals to that of humans, notably children who she knew from first-hand experience could be truly awful and offensive to each other.

Her parents had been relatively normal if that is a way to describe any humans.

Her mother worked at the local theatre on the bookstall for many years and her father had worked first as a carpenter and then selling life insurance. They had always worked for their money and that had instilled a strong work ethic in Morgan.

They had loved her very much and never wanted another child and for her part Morgan was very grateful for that. Morgan couldn't think of anything much worse than having a brother or sister and all the noise that went with that. She liked quiet, or silence even, preferably with just bird song to listen to.

It was a lovely childhood overall with fond memories of being taken to see many plays at the theatre and playing countless games of chess with her dad which he always let her win.

She had also dearly loved the many family pets which she had been brought up with including a tortoise, Russian hamsters, and her best friend Smokey the cat.

There had been the odd incident that had confused her even as a child though.

Morgan would have been about eight at the time when she was waiting at the pelican crossing to cross the busy main road on her way home from school when a large car transporter stopped to let her and a few other school children cross the road.

After she had crossed the road and the car transporter set off to continue on its journey Morgan had heard a distinct voice in her head say, "It's not safe!"

She looked down the road and saw some straps flapping loosely from behind the car transporter. It didn't look safe and a huge Mercedes looked not to be secured to the transporter anymore. As she looked at this in horror she tried to communicate, "It's not safe!" to the driver by staring at the back of the transporter and the now wobbling Mercedes. The hazard lights went on and the truck pulled over infuriating the car drivers behind it and as Morgan watched the driver get out and look at the back of the truck and the Mercedes she wondered if it was down to her that an accident had been avoided. The driver strapped the car securely to the trailer and although there were numerous people around he looked straight at Morgan who was a long way up the road by now and mouthed thank you to her. He then got back in the now safe transporter and Morgan pondered the event while pushing the peas around her plate when having her tea later that evening with her mum and dad.

Even at this young age she knew there was no real point in talking to them about the incident so she pondered the events while steering the peas into an orderly pile.

A couple of years later, when the incident with the car transporter was long forgotten, she was waiting to cross a road with speed bumps on when an old Suzuki 4x4 drove gently past her at a low speed and she looked at the spare wheel attached to the rear of the car because the cover had a nice picture of her horse jumping on it, she had felt a sense of foreboding and continued to watch the car as it crossed another speed bump.

The jolt had caused the spare wheel to fall off but luckily there wasn't a car immediately behind it. She stared as the wheel bounced down the road and then stared at a lamppost by the side of the road willing the wheel to come to rest there.

Sure enough the wheel came to a halt and propped itself against the lamppost. The driver of the car had not noticed what had happened and had driven on, but when he eventually realised it had come adrift from the car it would be safely propped up by the roadside for his collection where it was certain not to affect any other road users.

Morgan Fiona Martin often pondered these and a few other weird events which had taken place in her formative years, but now aged 44 she just accepted them as a part of her character and was grateful she had certain abilities which other people appeared not to possess.

She was a good looking woman and had aged well for her years with her thick red hair, faultless ivory skin, and big dark brown eyes; she was quite stunning in fact.

There didn't appear to be any history of weirdness in her family that she could see yet some days Morgan felt decidedly weird.

When very young and at primary school she had once voiced that there were birds in the background of the pictures hanging on the classroom wall and that she had liked watching them fly around. The teacher and the other kids wouldn't believe her and told her she was not seeing any such thing as it was impossible.

For a short time she had believed them, and in this time of disbelief there were no birds in the background of the pictures. It was dull and she missed them and sure enough when she convinced herself the birds were real and the people around her were wrong they had come back again. One robin even came to the forefront of a picture of fairies and put his head on one side while looking at her and tweeted his contentment to her. Morgan was thrilled to see him but never again bothered telling humans the truth of what she could see.

Morgan lived in Stratford-Upon-Avon now as she had done all her life. She loved the town and its culture and history and wouldn't want to live anywhere else in the world.

Since her parents had retired to a picture postcard cottage in Cornwall she had been more than happy living alone, except for Mally her beloved cat.

Things were subtly different now though, whilst her mum and dad had enjoyed a decade of happy retirement overlooking the sea and watching the boats coming into and going out of the harbour below them from their conservatory her dad was now alone, except for his cat Tabby.

Lennie claimed he was quite happy on his own but Morgan often worried about him and looked in the mirror often to check her dad and Tabby were managing alright.

She often saw Tabby gazing up lovingly at him while sitting on the newspaper he was trying to read, and the image always made her smile.

Morgan's mum Sylvie had died a year ago now. She had been in her eighties and very frail, but overall she had lived a long and happy life.

Morgan knew her mother was still with her and looking out for her. Ever since her death there had been a huge amount of robins sitting in the foreground of the pictures on her walls watching her intently and it was comforting, even if it looked a little odd when a robin had peered out at her from a picture of a Spitfire, which had seemed more than a bit out of context.

It had also been more than a little odd when after a quiet evening watching her Magic Flute DVD with Mally she had switched the television screen off only to find an image of a robin looking straight back at her with its head leaning slightly to one side and singing birdsong contentedly. Mally hadn't been at all impressed by that one and had sat glowering at the screen with his tail swishing vigorously behind him.

In her teenage years she had a couple of boyfriends and they were nice enough lads, but Morgan had never wanted to live with a fellow human being and certainly didn't want go get married and have children. In truth she had only had boyfriends in her youth because it was expected of her, she could quite happily not have bothered at all.

By now she was absolutely content as she was and much preferred her own company, or Mally's, than being with other people. She liked nothing more than sitting in front of the fire with Mally purring contentedly while she was reading a good book.

Mally was named after the Malleus Maleficarum: the hammer of witches. It was a little joke between them and it suited him as he was a black furry cat who would not look out of place on the back of a witch's broomstick and Morgan certainly possessed some qualities which could be seen as being akin to witchcraft or magic.

Morgan had read a few books on witchcraft and found the subject interesting, as she had found reading the Malleus Maleficarum interesting.

The Malleus Maleficarum is a treatise on the prosecution of witches, written in 1486 by Heinrich Kramer, a German Catholic clergyman. The book was first published in Germany in 1487.

The Malleus asserts that three elements are necessary for witchcraft: the evil intentions of the witch, the help of the Devil, and the Permission of God. The treatise is divided into three sections. The first section tries to refute critics who deny the reality of witchcraft, thereby hindering its prosecution. The second section describes the actual forms of witchcraft and its remedies. The third section is to assist judges confronting and combating witchcraft. However, each of these three sections has the prevailing themes of what is witchcraft and who is a witch.

The Malleus argues that women are more susceptible to demonic temptations through the manifold weaknesses of their gender. It was believed that they were weaker in faith and more carnal than men. It was claimed that most of the women accused as witches had strong personalities and were known to defy convention by overstepping the lines of proper female decorum.

Morgan found all this fascinating as it all inferred a woman perfectly ordinary most of the time as she was would stand out purely because of her powers and be different based on carnal lust, which was something that was certainly not anywhere near her list of priorities.

As she had been reading her book she had gazed out of the window and seen the reflection of a cat about to jump onto a bookcase in the reflection. This had nothing to do with special powers. She turned round and looking straight into Mally's eyes as he was about to pounce as she told him particularly sternly, "Don't you even think about it pal!" To which he grudgingly relaxed his stance and curled up on the arm of their purple Dralon settee.

The reflection did prompt another childhood memory though, especially when she looked up at the large picture of Desert Orchid jumping over a fence which was hung in its gilt frame over the fireplace. When she was about ten her dad had taken her for a day at the races. She had loved the beautiful creatures, but had felt a constant sense of fear for their safety.

As she had looked into a glass window by the pre-parade ring she saw the reflection of a beautiful grey horse that was being walked around it in circles behind her.

In the reflection she saw him trip over a hurdle but when she looked behind her the floor was flat. It must be a message she had thought even at that young age.

She looked the horse in his big beautiful eyes and willed him to be careful and pick his feet up. Windy Day snorted his agreement and understanding back to her and twenty minutes later he was led into the winner's enclosure having performed a career best and having jumped beautifully. Morgan looked on and the horse looked straight back at her and bowed his head respectfully, he had understood her perfectly.

When her mum had died last year when Morgan was forty-three, she had decided to get her one and only tattoo done. It was partly in acknowledgement of how quickly a life could disappear and also a part of her also wanted to ensure she would try to enjoy every day of the rest of her life to the full. The design was of five cats sitting on a broomstick and the wording underneath it read 'SUBFUSCOUS'.

This was all part of her new carpe diem school of thought.

It was the closest meaningful word that she could find that included the initials of all the cats which she had lived within the years prior to Mally.

It also suited her character as subfuscous means slightly dark, dusky, or sombre.

Not that she was glum, she was quite happy with her lot in life but it was a shame cats had such a short lifespan compared to humans and her individual qualities could be perceived as dark to people who did not know her and her good intentions.

Morgan had had a few jobs in her time. She had trained in health and safety, worked at the local council, and for the past five years had worked at the Stratford Chronicle.

Morgan was a talented artist and had been self-employed doing pet portraits at one stage but it simply hadn't paid enough for her to continue it.

She still painted as a hobby though and particularly liked surreal art using striking colours to bring her dreams and visions to life.

It was a pity; she had loved meeting the cats and dogs she had done portraits of but had been far less keen on dealing with their owners with their criticism, timescales, and unrealistic demands.

She had once been asked to paint a portrait of a three legged cocker spaniel in the later years of its life. True, it was a lovely friendly dog with a gentle nature and great sense of fun, but as a contestant for a beauty contest it would have been certain to have come last.

Of course her surreal art wasn't particularly surreal to her, she was just bringing colour and depth to the scenes that were natural in her own mind and sometimes dreams.

At the moment she was drawing the seven ages of man from the famous Jacques speech in Shakespeare's As You Like It and was envisaging some of the people she had come across over her time in the various roles it outlined as she drew them falling through an hour glass, obviously with a number of cats in the background:

At first the infant, mewling and puking in the nurse's arms, she saw herself as the baby in her mother's arms content, protected, and looked after.

And then the whining school-boy, with his satchel and shining morning face, creeping like a snail, unwillingly to school: That was Pogo Patterson surely, her best friend at primary school who had spent half his time sulking and whining.

And then the lover, sighing like a furnace, with a woeful ballad made to his mistress' eyebrow: Her ex-boyfriend Simon who was a nice lad who had looked a lot like Jon Bon Jovi with his long blond hair back in the eighties.

Then a soldier, full of strange oaths and bearded like the pard, jealous in honour, sudden and quick in quarrel, seeking the bubble reputation even in the cannon's mouth: Morgan didn't know any soldiers and couldn't understand why people fought each other so she had drawn this as a young Tony Blair, who had been so willing to let others fight and die because of his instructions.

And then the justice, in fair round belly with good capon lined, with eyes severe and beard of formal cut, full of wise saws and modern instances, and so he plays his part. That had to be Geoffrey the very vocal NUJ Union Rep at the Stratford Chronicle who loved listening to his own voice and always had some cause, or other, to stand up for.

The sixth age shifts into the lean and slipper'd pantaloon, with spectacles on nose and pouch on side, his youthful hose, well saved, a world too wide for his shrunk shank, and his big manly voice, 160 turning again toward childish treble, pipes and whistles in his sound. That had to be her lovely old dad, ever wise and always a true gentleman, she even drew in Tabby sitting next to him.

Last scene of all, that ends this strange eventful history, is second childishness and mere oblivion. That was an older wiser Morgan, she quite looked forward to it. She was calmer and happier now than at any earlier point in her life.

A rainbow was in the background of her work as well as comedy and tragedy masks and a number of birds looking on from over and above her characters.

She would use many colours and a great deal of time to finish the picture and bring her art to life.

She just wished she could have a more creative job at the Stratford Chronicle, she would love to review the plays at the theatre or cinema releases for them and longed for that job.

Her job was fine and paid very well, but she knew really that she ought to be doing something far more creative.

Still she might not have everything but she had her health, her beautiful cat Mally, and a large amount of luck and good fortune going for her. All was well.

Chapter Three

Mirror Mirror

Morgan arrived at the offices of the Stratford Chronicle at 10.05am precisely and was greeted harshly by her boss Rose who looked up at her and stated, "You're late," then continued to read whatever was on the desk in front of her.

Geoffrey, the ever present photographer, was just on his way out to a job when he heard the very limited discussion take place. He immediately took umbrage to Rose's comment and said cheerily as he opened the front door. "You really shouldn't talk to our best member of staff like that." And with that, he winked at Morgan and shut the door behind him.

Morgan knew that Geoffrey had just made the atmosphere even worse as Rose was jealous of Morgan and didn't even bother trying to disguise the fact at all.

Rose was a dumpy and very plain woman and was envious of Morgan's good looks, but what really grated with her was that Morgan made huge amounts of advertising sales without even needing to make an effort.

Morgan would just sit there chatting merrily away to her various clients the vast majority of which she was more than happy to talk to and people would just buy advertising space off her without her needing to push it on to them.

Morgan couldn't help it if people responded to her charm and suggestions, but while she was laughing and joking on the phone while still getting the sales in Rose would sit gloomily at the desk at the other end of the office being persistently told by most people she called that they were just not interested or they had gone off to deal with a rival newspaper.

Although Morgan knew she ought to be doing something more creative, she earned a large amount of commission in the job and it really didn't involve her making any effort at all.

She hung her coat up on the hat and coat stand in the corner of the office and could feel Rose's eyes glaring into her back.

She looked into the mirror on the wall next to it and didn't see Rose, anyway she was just a minor inconvenience to Morgan. She looked at the bottom left corner of the mirror and saw her Mally curled up on the settee with his head resting on a purple velvet cushion while snoozing merrily. She was always happy so long as she knew her house was safe and Mally was happy, that was pretty much all that mattered to her.

Rose was now shuffling the papers on her desk repeatedly and giving Morgan the silent treatment, which was fine by her, so she sat at her own desk and called Omar, the manager of the local Indian restaurant.

"Hi Omar, Morgan at the Chronicle here, just wondered if you've got that new copy ready yet that we were talking about last week?"

She had a pleasant few words with him and offered to pop around at lunchtime and pick it up. "Lovely Omar, I'll come over at lunchtime and collect it... Oh great, thanks, a free lunch would be lovely, I'll look forward to that...Yes, I'd love to try something off your new menu." Morgan didn't see Rose roll her eyes as she was listening in on the conversation.

She then happily phoned the local cinema. "Hi Paul, Morgan here, have you got next week's listings ready yet?" Paul and Morgan chatted away and Paul offered to fax the listings straight over to her and said she would love the new film Pressure which was coming out on Friday and starred Colin Radcliffe who he knew she liked. They often talked about the films which were showing and due out soon and occasionally such as now Paul would offer her a complimentary ticket "Oh, if you're sure Paul that would be great. Thanks very much, that's kind, I'll let you know what I think of it next time we have a chat. Cheerio for now."

When she put the phone down Morgan made herself and Rose coffee and the atmosphere seemed to thaw a little.

Geoffrey came back into the office so she made him a mug of tea while she was on her feet.

Morgan knew a grudging peace was taking place when Rose declared, "Your sales figures are looking brilliant this month," although she noted Rose couldn't actually look her in the eye while uttering the words, still it was progress of sorts.

Morgan made a few more calls around her usual clients and got the new café which had just opened by the river to advertise for the next month with the chronicle. When it came to lunchtime and Rose had already gone out of the office she decided to take Omar up on his offer and then pick up her complimentary ticket for the cinema so she could attend the matinee of the new thriller with Colin Radcliffe starring in it which was out on Friday. She did love a good thriller. She just hoped she could get to the end of the film without intuitively knowing how it ends.

She checked how Mally was in the mirror while putting her coat back on: He hadn't moved an inch was still snoozing happily. Morgan smiled at the image – She wanted to come back as a pampered house cat in the next life, it would sure beat working for a living.

To be fair she only needed to work part-time at the chronicle to earn a very good wage to live on with all of the commission she earnt. She would often potter around Stratford and have a coffee and a cake, or sometimes a wander around a gallery or museum, and nobody at the chronicle would bat an eyelid as her gentle excursions usually meant that she would persuade the café or gallery to advertise with them without even making an effort. She would just put it forward as an option and nine times out of ten they would think it was a great idea. Of course she chose to spend much of her free time simply snuggled up at home with Mally by her side and a good book. That was her idea of a really good time.

Morgan was now sitting in the near empty Taj Mahal rattling the ice cubes in the glass of fizzy water the waitress had placed in front of her. Omar bounded over to the table and placed the new menu in front of her with a stance and expression which showed he was immensely proud of it.

Morgan just hoped he had included a decent vegetarian option and was relieved when she noticed the Aloo Dum on the menu.

It was placed before her within ten minutes as was Omar's copy for advertising his new menu and she enjoyed a thoroughly lovely meal. She was even given some modak for pudding: sweet flour dumplings stuffed with coconut, jaggery, nutmeg and saffron. It was steamed to perfection. Omar explained this was a famous Indian dessert prepared during the festival of Ganesh Chaturthi.

When Omar went to take a telephone call Morgan flagged the waitress down who confirmed the modak was vegetarian.

It was always a bit inconvenient in restaurants, especially when the food was free, but there was no way Morgan could bear to eat an animal.

Ever since when she was very young and her dad had made her a fish finger sandwich which she had sat eating while lovingly watching Bill and Ben, with her pet goldfish swimming around their castle in circles and dancing around each other, that she had realised the hypocrisy of the act and in a moment of clarity she had decided never to eat meat of fish ever again.

It was now over thirty years ago since she had made that promise and she was still sticking to it diligently.

Omar came back to the table and asked Morgan how her meal was and she said honestly that it was lovely, which made him grin with pride.

Sitting down next to her briefly he then asked "and how is that beautiful cat of yours?" Everybody she spoke to for more than half an hour knew all about Mally and how much Morgan loved him.

Omar doted on his own cat too, a beautiful grey Korat girl called Shashthi which he explained means 'sixth.' There was an image of her in sitting in the corner of the picture of an Indian god, 'Ganesha', on a gold plaque beneath it which was opposite them on the wall. Shashthi sat in front of the elephant-deity which was riding a mouse, and looked calm, beautiful and most contented, but Morgan couldn't convey this to Omar of course. Omar explained that Shashthi is a Hindu folk goddess, venerated as the benefactor and protector of children, especially, as the giver of male child. She is also the deity of vegetation and reproduction and is believed to bestow children and assist during childbirth.

It was a lovely tale but Morgan thought it best not to explain that Mally was named after the Malleus Maleficarum and why that was for fear of causing offence.

Morgan herself wasn't named after Morgan le Faye, the powerful enchantress of Arthurian legend, which would have been hugely appropriate.

Morgan le Faye steals Excalibur's protective scabbard, which has been previously entrusted to her by King Arthur himself as he had trusted her the most. She takes it from the sleeping Arthur, and pursued by Arthur, she throws it into a lake; and this is the action that ultimately causes the death of Arthur, who would be otherwise protected in his final battle by the scabbard.

That was heady and worthy stuff indeed which would have appealed to Morgan's ego hugely.

But no, she was named Morgan because, from 1968, Morgan Cars were producing their new Morgan Plus 8 sports car with its powerful bubbling Rover V8 engine and since her dad had figured that there was now no way he could afford the bright red gleaming sports car which he would have loved now there was a baby on the way, he insisted on calling this daughter after the vehicle he now stood no chance of owning anytime soon.

Her mum had got her own way with her middle name which was Fiona, after her mother's best friend who had died just before Morgan was born when she was only forty-two. Sylvie had often said she had many of Fiona's traits such as imagination, creativity, and an interest in spirituality and interpreting dreams. Fiona also wrote a lot of poetry about fairies and elves which Morgan had loved reading.

When Morgan Fiona Martin was born at 8.00pm on Halloween 1970; fireworks lit up the sky with colour, as her mother had so often told her.

Anyway Morgan had finished her lovely meal and the lunchtime trade was starting to pick up in the restaurant, so she thanked Omar very much and quietly winked and bade farewell to the grey Korat girl Shashthi who was now curled up in the corner of the picture but still had one eye half open. She winked at the beautiful cat and thought she would pop around the corner and collect her free cinema ticket as it was only up the road. As she waited for Paul at the counter she looked at a poster advertising the latest release and made pleasant conversation with the young girl who was standing behind the popcorn machine. "What are those bluebells doing in a poster promoting a war film?" Morgan asked innocently.

But when the girl stared intently at the poster advertising American War Hero for moments and finally said, "I can't see any bluebells," Morgan was aware she should not have said anything. The girl continued to put popcorn in the machine and Morgan walked closer to the poster and saw that the image of a bunch of bluebells was indeed at the front corner of the poster but was definitely not supposed to be a part of it.

She was sure that she would find out what they represented in due course.

Paul bounded up to her and hugged her and they both chatted about the film coming out on Friday enthusiastically. "I don't know why that newspaper of yours doesn't get you to do the film reviews; you'd be the obvious choice and you know all about films."

Morgan couldn't agree more, but politely smiled at Paul and thanked him for the ticket.

She popped back to her office at the Chronicle and checked that Mally was safe at home while she was taking her coat off and looking in the mirror. He was safely curled up and snoozing contentedly.

"Hey witchy." Her old school friend Rita had just walked in to drop off a crossword entry. It was a statement and not a question so Morgan smiled at her as she went back out of the door.

Being born on Halloween had made Morgan the butt of many jokes and nicknames over the years but she took them good-naturedly and often joked about how much quicker journeys would be if she only had a broomstick.

In truth Morgan was more than happy to spend her entire time in Stratford but she would occasionally venture beyond to visit the theatre in Birmingham or in London to see a matinee performance. Always a matinee show as she wouldn't dream of leaving Mally on his own overnight.

She looked back in the mirror and saw the image of local theatre in the bottom corner, she presumed this was just because she was half-thinking of booking so see their new production, but just in case it wasn't she phoned their marketing department and asked if they wanted to place any adverts in this week's chronicle. "That's bizarre," said Zoe the marketing manager. "I was just going to ring you. I thought we might run a competition to win a pair of tickets to our new production of The Jew of Malta. Bizarre."

Bizarre was Zoe's favourite word. "Great Zoe, just let me know when the copy is ready and I'll pop down and collect it. See you in a bit."

As she went to put the phone down she heard the words, "Sure, bizarre."

As Geoffrey put the kettle on and asked Morgan if she fancied a coffee, Morgan got a slight feeling of unease. It was as though she knew he would injure himself somehow if she didn't intervene so she told him to sit down and that she would make the drinks which he duly did because he was intrinsically lazy. Morgan didn't know what she had averted by this intervention but the feeling of unease was now gone and she knew Geoffrey would be safe.

After drinking her coffee and collecting the copy from the theatre Morgan strolled home to her beloved furry friend. She was looking forward to a night in with him cuddled up together watching the soap operas and then off to bed together.

After a couple of whisky and milks, and a snivel through the latest romantic break up in Corrie, Mally and Morgan were back under the duvet snoozing. All of the robins in the pictures had gone to roost much earlier in the evening and Morgan happily snuggled up with her pal and dreamt about Fiona, her mum's spiritual and quirky friend.

She looked over the bed from above just the once during the night, but knew she was not going anywhere as she looked down on the intertwined Mally around herself as she happily dreamt of poetry about fairies and elves with Mally purring softly in her arms. A lovely image of the fairy queen Titania came into her dreams with flowing long blond hair, she was dressed in a beautiful azure blue floating gown with a bright pink aura surrounding her. Morgan thought that if she could remember the image when she awoke it could be the subject of her next painting. This was the sort of stuff her mum's friend Fiona constantly wrote about and painted pictures of, as her mother had so often told her. Maybe she still lived on through the power of dreams. Still when she had seen her roots from above they hadn't half looked grey, she would have to get the dye out in the near future and do something about that.

Chapter Four

A Date to Remember

Morgan sat on her purple Dralon settee with Mally reading a copy of The Stage newspaper. She was checking what new musicals and plays would be showing on the day of her birthday. It fell on a Saturday this year and there was no way she was going to navigate a busy city on a Saturday afternoon so she was thinking of attending a matinee on Thursday 29th of October in either London or Birmingham.

She had already seen most of the big ones which were still showing. She had loved Phantom, Les Miserables, and Cats, and was totally awestruck by Wicked, especially the Defying Gravity song just before the interval which was amazing, but her all-time favourite had to be Evita with its beautiful songs and music and the sheer power running through it at times.

She noticed a new production would be staged at The Adelphi in London and put a circle around the advert with the intention of ringing their box office in the near future.

Putting the paper down beside her, she then looked at the very nearly completed competition magazine crossword which was where she had left that page open on the coffee table before her.

He eyes kept being drawn to C3. Not the question or even the answer, C3 was clearly supposed to mean something to her; but right now she didn't understand what.

She thought about London and the hustle and bustle of the place, but she did love Evita so much and always insisted on having an excursion for her birthday. She would soon forget about the crowds and the travelling when she was sitting in the sumptuous auditorium of the Adelphi with its sumptuous red velvet seats and glorious architecture.

No time like the present. She jotted down the phone number from the advert in The Stage and rang the Adelphi box office from the phone in her hall.

As she dialled the number an image of a pressurised water pistol appeared in the bottom left corner of the mirror as she waited for someone to pick up the phone at the other end. "Hi there, could I please book a ticket for the showing of Evita on the 29th October matinee?" She was asked if she had a preference for stalls or circle. "I'd like seat C3 in the stalls if it is available please." The lady at the other end confirmed the seats availability. "Do you know who will be playing Che and Evita yet?" She was told both of the roles were still being cast as far as the box office lady knew. So that was it, done and booked. She sat back down next to Mally and he gave her a knowing look. She hugged him and assured him it was only for one day and she would be back by the evening and promised him a special supper when she got back.

Morgan pondered for a minute what on Earth the pressurised water pistol was about, but decided that thinking about it was unlikely to give her any answers as it was such a random object.

She took her diary out of her handbag and by the 29th October wrote, 'Evita 2.30pm C3'.

Why the C3 was significant she still did not know, she had subconsciously written that bit down.

She could hear a couple arguing and a woman crying and glanced at the telly to see what it was about, but there was a programme about hummingbirds on which was certainly not the source of the commotion in fact it was rather lovely.

The green and red hummingbird looked beautiful close up, but all of a sudden while watching it, Morgan felt a great sorrow wash over her. Not her own sorrow but somebody else's.

For some reason she knew that two children were involved as well as a desperate man. She could picture none of them clearly and had no idea who they were or where they lived but the sorrow and desperation were tangible.

She gave Mally a little stroke and, because the feeling was so powerful and acute, she went to see if there were any clues as to what this was about in the mirror which hung in her hall.

Two beautiful but sad looking little girls looked back at her out of the mirror, their eyes red from crying. Behind them was the exterior of a lovely terraced house but still Morgan had no idea what the visibly upset children had to do with her.

She glanced back at the television where the hummingbird was still flapping around looking beautiful and her feelings went back to being calm and quite happy with her lot in life if a little confused.

She went into the kitchen and made herself some cheese on toast and put some chicken slices in Mally's bowl. She then curled up on the settee in her tatty old grey but very comfy tracksuit to watch the rest of the nature documentary. Mally was keeping an interested eye on the exotic birds too but that was for very different reasons.

Morgan loved days like this, just pottering around the house and not having to speak to anyone, she could happily go for days on end without bothering with people. She finished her cheese on toast and put her plate on the floor then settled back into the settee for a gentle snooze.

As she dozed off she saw images of London which included the Houses of Parliament with Big Ben and Hamleys, the toyshop on Regents Street where she and her mum had one traipsed all around before drinking hot chocolate with marshmallows together in the café that was a part of the shop.

Morgan was awoken from her slumber by Mally jumping onto her stomach and kneading her sweatshirt while staring straight into her eyes and purring loudly.

The chicken slices had obviously hit the spot and he settled down after a stoke on the head for a nice relaxing afternoon slumber.

In her half-sleep she saw her own diary open on the week of her birthday this year as well as images of what she presumed was still London, but were in an area she didn't believe she had ever been to. At the corner of a row of expensive looking Georgian terraced houses was a sign which read 'Lavender Crescent' and a little further down the houses she paused in front of number 13.

Looking back out at her from the downstairs bay window was one of the little girls she had seen earlier in the mirror, but she now had a smile on her little face making her look much prettier. She had her right arm draped around a beautiful white Samoyed dog. Assuming this was a dream and she could not be seen by the girl Morgan walked up the stairs to the house for a closer look. The girl appeared unconcerned and unknowing, but the dog looked across at her pointedly knowing full well she was there. He had a disc attached around his neck displaying his name, 'Snowbell', and he looked like the most lovely white teddy bear close up. He was stunning with his pure white fur and black lined green eyes and was obviously fond of the girl, who's arm was casually draped around him.

She stirred from her snooze and put an arm around Mally before changing position slightly. There was nothing remarkable about thinking about London when she had just booked to go there and the dreaming about the diary dates didn't surprise her for the same reason but something was definitely drawing her towards this family and their London home and there would doubtless be a reason.

She drifted back off to sleep with a powerful smell of lavender filling her senses and again saw the sign for Lavender Crescent, but this time a little closer up so that she could see the smaller writing running across the top of the sign which read Borough of Kensington and Chelsea. She was again drawn back to house number 13, but all was quiet now and neither the girl nor the dog was in sight. As she turned around she saw a huge amount of lavender bushes on the opposite side of the road and pondered for a moment how delightful but powerful the smell emitting from them was.

That was it though for now, nap over and all seamed well in the World. She did pick up a pen though and wrote on the pad on her coffee table '13 Lavender Crescent'. It surely had some significance.

She put a circle around the number 13. It had always been a lucky number to her.

There are 13 witches in a coven, but Morgan didn't really possess team spirit to give that one a go.

She had tried to read tarot cards in the past, but wasn't particularly good at it. She had actually thought up quite a good idea for a musical where periodically a large tarot card would fall from above the stage and therefore change the circumstances, relationships, emotions, and music for the cast below. The cards would have to be read for their meanings while taking into account the relationship between the falling card with the card which landed before it and the one landing on the stage after it. It wasn't a bad idea but Morgan had never learnt to read or write music so it was all a bit half-baked.

The dabble into the tarot had taught her that the thirteenth card, which is 'Death', is actually an auspicious card meaning positive changes to people who believe in the tarot.

To Pagan's, which Morgan considered herself loosely to be, the number 13 is lucky and it also corresponds to the number of full moons in a year.

She stopped circling the number 13 and looked at her beautiful picture of Desert Orchid captured mid-jump on her living room wall wondering if the tale of 13 Lavender Crescent was likely to be a lucky one.

At the forefront of the picture were a couple of robins which seemed happy enough and were singing their birdsong contentedly, but between them and the race horse was the beautiful Samoyed Snowbell from earlier sitting calmly next to a rather agitated and twitchy looking dove which looked anything but peaceful.

Well, not having a clue what she could do about a seemingly upset dove, Morgan flicked through the TV channels with the remote control and settled back to watch a repeat of the film Billy Elliot. It didn't matter that she'd seen it umpteen times before, it was still a brilliant story. She also picked up the competition magazine from the coffee table and completed all the crosswords and puzzles in it while watching the film and eating a bag of salt and vinegar crisps - who said she couldn't multi-task?

After sniffing at the ending of the film, with the powerful music from Swan Lake making her snivel even more, Morgan got up and rattled some turkey biscuits into Mally's bowl and poured herself a large whisky and milk.

If only every day could be a relaxed, slobbing around day like today, she would be happy.

Looking out of the window while finishing her drink she looked out at a glittering starry sky full of bright stars and with a full moon appearing to guard them imperially, it was utterly beautiful. Underneath the sky shrouded in the moonlight a lone fox was wandering across the road on his nightly rounds, but other than that all was calm with not a person in sight.

Mally sat on the arm of the settee watching her and knowing it was coming up to their bedtime. All of the robins in the pictures had long since gone to roost, and Snowbell and the dove had now vacated her artwork. Morgan looked at the wonderful stars and then into the glass window which was reflecting her beautiful boy sitting on the settee watching her and she knew that all was well in her world.

Polishing off her drink and giving Mally a ruffle of the fur on his head she decided it was their bedtime. She switched the living room light off and had a quick look in the hall mirror before climbing the stairs to bed. The two girls were back again, but this time in the background behind them was a man and a woman who were arguing and looking upset. Morgan guessed these were the girl's parents. There was a sense of gloom about them all. Words then came into her head as if she had the man in the mirror standing right beside her saying them, "I know I've got to tell her," followed by, "I was desperate, still am, and I don't know what to do."

Morgan wasn't scared by this and didn't expect to be seeing this man in the near future but she knew that one day they would meet. He seemed weak, scared, and despondent, but Morgan had a feeling she wouldn't be required to do anything about it tonight so she went for a long undisturbed night's sleep with Mally cuddled up next to her on the duvet.

She dreamt of the beautiful moon shining on the front door with the number 13 on. When she awoke the next morning a strong smell of lavender filled the bedroom, but just as quickly it was gone as she got dressed in her cords and purple jumper and pulled on her red cowboy boots. She would do a half day at the office, sell the last remaining advertising space before this week's Stratford Chronicle was put to bed and should be back at home in time to watch Judge Rinder.

One of Morgan's more peculiar traits was to consistently find gay men to be attractive and her latest crush from a distance was the judge Rob Rinder.

In truth, she was not interested in men at all romantically, she much preferred the company of cats but it was a good programme.

It was a shame sometimes when his lovely face was obscured by a robin looking out at her from the TV set, but she could live with it, to be fair she found the robins to be rather lovely too and certainly calming and reassuring.

A morning in the same office as Rose was about long enough, after about three hours she would be grateful for her own company again.

Chapter Five

The Spencers

Roy Spencer had been a moderately successful guy, in a plod along kind of way, all of his working life.

Now in his late forties, he had originally trained as an accountant but never practiced as one. He got his first job as a temporary cashier in the Chelsea branch of the Norton Bank nearly thirty years ago and had been there ever since.

It was hardly a meteoric rise to the top. He was made permanent staff after six months and had worked as a cashier there for twenty years, following that before reaching the heady post of assistant manager five years ago and then being manager for the last three years.

Roy had never really been what you might call ambitious. His parents had instilled a strong work ethic in him from a young age and he had always been of the mind-set that you have to work hard for your money and he had done that, but in truth he only got the post of assistant manager because the previous one had retired and he was the longest serving member of staff and he had only then been promoted to manager when Bill Jones who had hired him all those years ago had a stoke while feeding the ducks in the park and died by the duck pond.

It was assumed that Roy would take over for the interim period after Bill's demise, but somehow he had just been left to get on with the job he had never even applied for.

He had received a pay rise and all the staff knew him as the manager, but nobody had actually bothered interviewing him or asking him if he wanted the job.

Rumours had been bumbling throughout the bank staff for some time now about branch closures and a push on internet banking and Roy had largely kept his head down and ignored them. He hated the internet and if he could get away with still doing his job with a pen and paper he would.

He was not progressive and nobody had offered him training regarding internet banking, so he had quietly just continued running the branch in a friendly but old fashioned way. He liked dealing with customers face to face, he was good at it and the staff seemed to respect him, but recently he had noticed the number of customers at the branch had diminished considerably and a rather attractive but unsmiling young woman called Nina had been sent to the branch from the head office in Oxford to monitor customer transactions and product sales within the branch.

That roughly translated to getting in Roy's way when he was trying to do his job and asking for various statistics to enable her to produce an in depth report into the long term feasibility of customer facing banking, whilst looking into alternative methods of service delivery better suited to a modern and evolving clientele with different needs and expectations from their bank.

In other words, Roy's days at the bank would appear to be seriously numbered, which scared him to death as he had an expensive wife, an expensive house, and two very expensive young daughters at home.

Maxine Spencer was a very good looking woman and if anything looked better in her early forties than she had ten years ago. Her long hair was dyed a bright blonde and was full of bouncing curls and her ivory skin was glowing with radiance, but her piece de résistance was her long immaculately manicured nails which were usually vividly coloured with gemstones stuck on to them creating a dazzling effect.

For years she had visited a nail technician once a week but eventually she had a lightbulb moment, and having received so many compliments on her own nails wherever she went, she had decided to train herself as a nail technician and had set up a small but quite successful business which she ran from a downstairs spare room at 13 Lavender Crescent. In fact, it had been Roy's study but he rarely used it so she had taken it over and given it a revamp with plush red velvet chaise lounges on a black shag pile carpet with mirrored walls to show off her handiwork to full effect. It looked like a stylish upmarket salon and her increasing number of upmarket clients looked very stylish indeed when they left after being pampered and beautified.

True, she had some quite demanding clients who were used to dolling out orders and getting their own way because of their moneyed existences, but this was an upmarket area of London and the tips she received were very generous indeed and she had even become firm friends with a couple of her much nicer clients which was great as she hadn't made any real friends since she had her children. It was lovely to have a glass of wine and a chat while doing Sandy or Lynda's nails, they even brought a bottle of Chardonnay along to their nail appointments sometimes.

Maxine loved her girls but welcomed a proper grown up conversation sometimes.

She had even taken to inviting Jehovah's Witnesses in for a chat when they knocked on the door, the last time that happened was mid-afternoon on a weekday when, over a cup of coffee, she had been told all about what the bible says about the need to work and be proud of what you are doing in the name of God.

It was only after she had closed the door behind the two middle-aged women that she smiled at the irony of the conversation, led by the two women who were obviously not in any sort of gainful employment on a weekday afternoon.

They would doubtless be back around Easter time when Maxine was celebrating the creation of milk chocolate and the Easter Bunny to rain on her parade and tell her all about what Jesus died for, but at least it was a proper conversation of sorts if a little one-sided.

Last month the local Tory Councillor had knocked on the door and Maxine invited the woman in for a chat and a coffee. Margaret Poulter was more her sort of guest as she had always voted Conservative and agreed with most of their principles. She had also agreed to post some campaigning literature around the local area for Margaret and after the fifteen-minute chat had almost been persuaded to stand for election herself in due course. The idea boosted her confidence to no end and she had an interest in current affairs, so why not? But what about the children?

Titania and Amber were her life because they had to be, not because Maxine particularly wanted it that way. They had taken away her youth and her freedom and made constant demands on her time and generally drove her round the bend with their whinging, screeching, and untidiness.

If only Maxine could turn back time and make a completely different set of decisions. She had been a young woman with no career path whatsoever when she had met Roy. He was pleasant looking, chivalrous, and kind. All she had wanted then was to settle down with a man who would look after her and to have a child. As an only child herself, she had only wanted the one and maybe a cat or dog as well, so when she had found out she was expecting twins the whole plan fell apart and she was terrified by the idea.

In the first few years of their courting and marriage, Roy took Maxine to the opera and the ballet and educated her as she had never seen either before and she had loved it. Now if he put his classical music on when he came in from work it just irritated her.

They had dined out often and laughed and conversed together freely, but now they had slid into a routine of only conversing over bills and school fees and hardly ever laughing at all.

Maxine blamed the kids for the change in her marriage. She knew she was being unfair, but Roy worshiped the girls and they adored him, it was as if she was just there to feed them and deliver and collect them from their ballet classes. Even then she saw them look at her with disappointment for not being their dad when collecting them. Maxine wasn't even sure she loved the girls, she knew she was supposed to but in actual fact she by far preferred the company of her dog Snowbell, he was loyal and gorgeous and had a quiet intelligence which couldn't be seen in her gobby girls.

Maxine felt she was living life in the opposite direction of travel. When she was young she wanted a nice husband, a nice house, and a nice child, but now she wanted to laugh, have fun, and be successful at something in her own right.

She had probably married Roy too quickly because if she had left it longer before she did she would have realised what a dull, unambitious, and homely person he was. After the girls were born they stopped going to the theatre and hardly ever went to a restaurant. Roy just seemed happy to come home from the bank and read a newspaper or a book and to read his girls a bedtime story, before tucking them in and resuming his book while Maxine would appear to have become invisible in his world.

She had taken to curling up on the settee knackered after looking after the girls all day while he was at work with the dog and a large glass of wine, she was too tired to even bother saying anything about it so they had slipped into an uncomfortable routine of living in the same house whilst hardly speaking to each other.

On the mantelpiece in a gilt frame was a large photograph of them on their wedding day which was posed outside the entrance to St Milburga's Church in Chelsea.

Roy looked handsome in his black dinner suit with pink tie and Maxine looked beautiful in a huge puff of a white satin wedding gown with her face beautifully made-up and framed perfectly by blonde ringlets. They looked and were a very good looking couple, but what always stood out to Maxine when she looked at the photo was the adoring looks they were giving each other, at the time it was as though nothing in the world mattered to them but each other and there was such hope and promise for the future in that one captured look.

Perhaps she was being unfair, she lived in a lovely house which she couldn't imagine being able to pay for without Roy as she wasn't really that good at very much, including being a mother, she didn't have to work for a living and the kids were now away at boarding school for a lot of the time, so maybe she might make a concerted effort to get things back on track with Roy, she would see if she could be bothered sometime later.

The girls first couple of years had been hard on the marriage. It was a big enough shock having twins in the first place and all the work that created with Roy evading most of that as he was at work in his nice quiet bank, but they had been such sickly children and if one hadn't had an infection of some sort the other one had. The crescendo came in stereo at one point when they had both had an ear infection at the same time and screamed and wailed at the top of their voices.

Maxine had tried her best, but had to get away from the noise emanating from the children and had sat at the patio table in the back garden listening to the birds in the relative quiet with a large glass of chardonnay when Roy had come home from his day at the bank and gone straight up to the girls' bedroom where they had calmed down almost immediately in his presence. He had always been a hero to Titania and Amber.

It had never been discussed why she was drinking wine in the garden while her kids had been screaming the house down, but Roy was so mild mannered he had just done what was necessary at the time and that in itself addressing the elephant in the room.

Still, life was a bit better all-round now, Roy was going to drop the girls at their little friend's birthday party later, so at least she would be shot of the whinging brats for a while and her first go at running a business would appear to be going remarkably well.

Not only was she making a bit of money of her own from the nails, but her godmother had died recently and she had inherited a few quid thereafter, so right now she felt like a woman of means, she might even get more involved in politics, she could fancy herself as a Conservative Councillor one day.

Roy was looking at the heavy oak door which was firmly closed as he sat in the corridor of his own bank waiting to be escorted in to meet a disciplinary panel. He had been told he could bring a union representative to support him but had declined the offer.

He just sat staring at the closed door thinking of the beautiful faces of his wife and children and wondering how his entire life could have turned upside down so quickly.

He would no longer be able to pay for the house, the kids very expensive schooling, or even their precious ballet classes unless he could find a way of making some decent money in the very near future.

Far worse than being made redundant for being a Luddite and forgoing his carriage clock and retirement package, Roy had made a monumentally stupid decision based on desperation and was now waiting for three people he did not know and did not want to know to decide that fate would befall him. He presumed he was still sitting in this corridor to make him sweat and see the error of his ways, but all Roy could really focus on was his house, the kids, and the school fees and how on earth he could continue to pay for them all.

He had been cashing up two days ago when suddenly after years of looking after other people's money and handling it constantly he had found himself holding a bundle containing five thousand pounds and instead of putting it in the safe found himself putting it in his inside jacket pocket.

Roy had never stolen even a lollipop in his life and over the many years at the bank millions of pounds must have passed through his hands, but Roy simply had to pay the latest bill for the school fees and didn't know when he was likely to earn any proper money again. He only knew about numbers and statistics and hadn't got a clue about what he was going to do by way of gainful employment in the near future.

The door creaked opened and a sullen looking Nina said the panel were ready for him, and then awkwardly stood in the doorway while he entered the room and shut the door behind her with the sound of her high heels teetering off back down the corridor breaking the silence that followed.

Two young men in smart grey suits and a dolly bird in a low cut black sequinned top sat behind the huge oak desk with its green leather inlaid panel. They nodded they were aware that he had entered the room and the younger looking man ushered for Roy to take a seat before them, which he duly did feeling like he was being treated as a recalcitrant child.

Eventually, Gareth, the younger man, introduced Trisha and Karl and explained why Roy had been summoned before them. It was made abundantly clear that he would forgo his redundancy package as he had stolen the five thousand pounds, which doing the quick mental arithmetic meant he had done himself out of around fifty grand, this lot should really be jumping up and down thanking him for his downright stupidity, he had saved Norton Bank at least forty-five thousand pounds, but no, he was going to have to listen to a lecture from these kids and make sure he looked suitably contrite.

Gareth, who he had laid eyes on for the first time just five minutes ago, assessed correctly that Roy had acted out of desperation and a feeling of being surplus to requirements with his redundancy from Norton being just around the corner. "Uncanny," he thought to himself, the guy should write self-help books.

Trisha said that due to his crime being totally out of character and taking into account Roy's hitherto unblemished work record at the bank the panel were prepared not to involve the police so long as Roy's desk was clear by the end of the day and he did not approach any members of the company further to his dismissal. It was also make clear no references would be supplied by the bank to any future employers Roy might approach.

Roy grudgingly thanked the panel for their time and decision and wandered out of the office stunned by how quickly his life had descended into this mess, helped along by his own total stupidity and embarrassment.

He cleared his desk and put his lovely gold Cross pen, which Maxine had bought him for Christmas many years ago, into his inside jacket pocket. He picked up his rarely used briefcase and tossed his leather bound notebook inside and stood back to survey his empire one last time. The staff had scuttled off and left him to it and as he made it to the revolving front door he had spent hours of his life in the tears started to flow. He couldn't go home yet so he walked around the block and through the park envying the ducks their seemingly uncomplicated lives. What the hell was he going to do now and how could he possibly tell Maxine what he had been up to?

Chapter Six

A Drink, a Book and a Fly

Morgan was pottering around the Marlowe Museum in Stratford. It was a beautiful old building and had such character and history about it.

There was nobody else around except the pretty blonde girl standing behind the counter surrounded by a number of guide books and information leaflets.

Morgan smiled at her and the girl smiled back saying she hated being in the building when it was empty, loved her job but the building creaked and made noises when there was no one around.

Morgan walked across the huge tapestry rug which covered the centre of the room and as she did so she shivered as she felt she was being pulled at from underneath the floor.

The girl must have sensed her unease and said with little emotion, "You're walking across the priest hole, it's sealed now but it used to lead to the church."

"I just had a horrible feeling as if I was being pulled into it," exclaimed Morgan who was now looking at the ornate patterned rug as if it could give her some answers when clearly it could not.

Katie, as she introduced herself to Morgan while putting out her hand to shake it, explained that a priest hole is the term given to hiding places for priests which were built into many of the principal Catholic houses in England during the period when Catholics were persecuted by law in England, from the beginning of the reign Queen Elizabeth in 1558.

Morgan went back to where she had been standing on the rug and felt that somebody had been trapped inside the hole. It wasn't something pulling her down, it was more as though somebody wanted her to pull them up and out of the hole. It was a very odd sensation.

According to Katie's boss Eric, who was away today, the effectiveness of priest holes was demonstrated by their success in baffling the exhaustive searches of the 'pursuivants', or priest hunters, described in contemporary accounts of the searches. Search-parties would bring with them skilled carpenters and masons and try every possible expedient, from systematic measurements and soundings to the physical tearing down of panelling and pulling up of floors. It was common for a rigorous search to last for a week and for the 'pursuivants' to go away empty handed, while the object of the search was hidden the whole time within a wall's thickness of his pursuers, or in this case under the floor. He might be half-starved, cramped, sore with prolonged confinement, and almost afraid to breathe lest the sound should throw suspicion upon the particular spot where he was immured. Sometimes a priest could die from starvation or by lack of oxygen.

"I studied the History of this place myself," said Katie proudly, "and I've asked lots of questions about this building: it would seem a Catholic priest called John Taylor, his wife Caroline and their daughter Evelyn lived in this house from 1556 onwards. I don't know what happened to them though as records are very unclear about it."

"I know what happened to Evelyn," said Morgan earnestly and sadly with tears starting to roll down her cheeks. "She was put in the priest hole for her own protection but could never get back out again as her parents were captured."

Katie didn't argue with or ridicule Morgan as she walked around to join her and handed her a tissue. After a while she broached, "When I've been in this building in the early evening I've heard banging from in here and sometimes sobbing and the occasional scream."

The two women just looked at each other, but as Morgan looked slightly beyond Katie she saw, clearly standing against a portrait of a previous resident on the far wall, there stood a beautiful but filthy little girl with long blonde hair and bright blue eyes wearing a look of serenity about her now that her story had been told. "Turn around very slowly," said Morgan and Katie did as she was asked. The little girl waved at them both and smiled and faded into the picture and the wall as Morgan and Katie waved and smiled back at her.

Long moments passed in silence, but a friendship had been borne between Morgan and Katie over a most peculiar experience. Katie put the kettle on and made them both a strong coffee. Morgan couldn't even be bothered suggesting the museum should advertise with the Chronicle which was loosely the point of her visit there in the first place.

As Morgan took a slow stroll back to the office she popped into the Preston Bakery and bought a couple of chocolate eclairs, she was having a moment of generosity of spirit and thought she would take one back for Rose.

As Mr. Preston served her with an amicable smile, he asked if he could put an advert in the paper to promote his new range of pasties. "No problem, have you got an advert already designed?" Reaching across to the shelf under the till he picked up a leaflet and handed it across to her. "That's good enough quality to lift from, would you like a 5 X 2 in the 'Eating out in and around Stratford section'?" Thinking for a minute, he replied that would be great and he also refused to take any payment for the eclairs.

She walked into the Chronicle office and handed a thoroughly miserable looking Rose the éclair declaring, "Pressie for you," which made Rose smile and look infinitely more attractive than usual, she then went to hang her coat up and check how Mally was doing in the mirror. He was looking out of the window at a huge pigeon which was taking liberties by sitting just inches away from him on the other side of the glass pane, causing him to glare and swish his tail about in disgust which was not upsetting the bird one jot as it obviously knew Mally couldn't get at it. The image made Morgan smile. She then looked up and saw a sprig of lavender in the top right corner of the mirror. It must be to do with the house in London she thought, but other than that she still knew nothing.

She sat at her desk and enjoyed her complimentary chocolate éclair then booked in the Preston Bakery for an advert on page 6 of this week's paper.

Rose made them both a cup of coffee, which obviously translated to 'thanks for the éclair' without actually having to say thank you to Morgan which would be inconceivable, and they both chatted amicably about what news stories would be in this week's Chronicle; local politics, the council's lack of planning policy, and charity work with kids having their hair shaved off, it was hardly cut and thrust news.

Morgan made a mental note to bring cake back to the office more often as it made for a much improved and calmer working environment. She could even like the new improved recently fed version of Rose.

She phoned a couple of the cafes in Stratford and one of them decided to take out an advert to promote their specialty herbal infused teas, so deciding she had done her bit for the Chronicle and work relations for one day Morgan put her coat on, bade Rose farewell, and went home to sooth Mally after his run in with the pigeon which had obviously perturbed him.

It was a fifteen-minute walk home and the sun was shining although not giving off much warmth. Morgan had bought a pack of chicken slices en route to placate her faithful friend as well as a bottle of whisky for herself. As she put the key in the lock and walked into the hall Mally gave her a lazy meow from the settee with one eye open and as she looked into the mirror she saw an abundance of robins looking back at her and smelt a waft of Panache perfume. She smiled and said, "Hello Mum."

After putting the chicken slices into Mally's bowl, which judging by the loud purring noise certainly met with his approval, Morgan poured herself a whisky and milk. It was a bit early but it had already been an eventful day.

As she switched the telly on and snuggled down on the settee to read a chapter of her thriller, she glanced up to see what programme was on and was surprised to see underneath the news headlines a Jack Russell dog looking out of the screen plaintively at her with big brown soulful eyes.

Morgan made a mental note to go easy on the whisky as she had a strong feeling she might have to go floating somewhere after the dog later.

Mally settled down happily next to her as she read about a particularly grotesque murder committed by gangsters in the East End of London, but its severity lost impact due to the loud purring emitting from her friend.

It was no good trying to concentrate for more than another chapter as a plaintive whimpering noise was forthcoming from the image of the Jack Russell now sitting at the bottom of the television screen as if waiting expectantly.

"Well, Mally," said Morgan as she closed the book and placed it back on the coffee table, "it looks as if I can do something about this little fellow now and then we can have a quiet night in together, either that or I risk being pulled out of bed to do it later. I'll go with option A pal." And she gave him a ruffle of the fur on his head.

She walked across to the telly and looked intently at the image of the dog. "OK then, who are you, where are you, and what am I supposed to be doing about you?"

Mally put his head on one side and looked at Morgan as if she were an idiot for asking such questions of the image of the dog and actually expecting answers, but he had seen his mum do many strange things over their years together.

Morgan squinted at the screen and saw an image of Meon Hill behind the dog and also saw the now clearly visible tag around his neck read 'Bruno'.

"OK Bruno, I'll be there shortly, worry not."

With that she switched the telly off and gave Mally a drink of milk as she felt guilty for going out again so soon. She promised him she would be back as soon as possible and put her coat back on and wandered back down town to the bus stop.

It was broad daylight and she would have no chance of floating the six miles to her destination without being seen.

She handed over her £2.00 to the bus driver and started the stop start journey which would take in a number of pretty Warwickshire villages before disembarking at Lower Quinton which sat at the foot of Meon Hill.

Morgan then gazed up at the beautiful hill which was enshrouded with history. It was said to be a meeting place for a coven of witches for many years with tunnels running throughout the hill for use by the witches.

It was also the site of the infamous murder of Charles Walton, who lived from 12 May 1870 until his murder in 14 February 1945, a resident of Lower Quinton, who was found murdered at a farm known as The Firs, situated on the slopes of Meon Hill. Chief Inspector Robert Fabian was asked to lead the investigation into Walton's death but failed to gather sufficient evidence to charge anyone with the murder. The case has earned considerable notoriety because some believe Walton was killed as a blood sacrifice, or as part of a witchcraft ceremony, or maybe, because he was suspected of being a witch himself. However, it is known that the chief suspect was the manager of The Firs, a man named Alfred John Potter, for whom Walton was working on the day he died. It is the oldest unsolved murder on the Warwickshire Police records.

For many years alternative theories have been circulating:

Charles Walton could have been a witch whose powers, such as his ability to cast the evil eye, were feared by some villagers. Moreover, it was claimed he kept Natterjack toads as pets and used these to 'blast' the fields of local farmers, driving them across their land and blighting their crops and livestock. The failure of the 1944 harvest and the death of Potter's heifer on 13 February are just two examples. Because of this, it could have been decided that he had to die and he may have been the victim of a ritualistic murder, killed in such a way that his blood would soak into the ground and replenish the soil's fertility.

It was very odd that Charles Walton was killed on Candlemas Day under the old calendar, which also happened to be the pagan festival of Imbolc. The belief was that the weather on that day held the key to weather patterns over the months to come. There was a perceived link between Candlemas and Imbolc and the success of the forthcoming harvest and since Charles Walton was blamed for the failure of the previous harvest, there could maybe be some logic in his murder occurring on that day, who knows.

Even as late as 1945, the residents of Quinton believed that phantom black dogs roamed the area and were a harbinger of death. Fabian himself wrote that he had encountered a black dog while walking at dusk on Meon Hill. The dog ran past him and shortly afterwards he met a local boy walking in the same direction. He asked the boy if he was looking for his dog, but when Fabian mentioned the animal's colour, the boy turned a deathly pale and fled in the opposite direction.

The hill had a quiet calmness and air of mystique and even belonging about it for Morgan as she looked up at it admiring its beauty, serenity, and significance. It held her attention with its power.

Stopping at the NAAFI for a can of cherry coke she walked along the path leading to the hill and along its crest looking for Bruno and what she was supposed to be doing about him.

She hadn't got far when the near silence she was walking in was broken by a sobbing sound and a man with a loud voice shouting, "Come on fella, time to go home."

Morgan walked towards them and asked if she could be of any help.

Cathy and Mike, as they introduced themselves, had been walking their dog when about an hour ago he had chased off after a rabbit. They had been searching for him ever since and feared Bruno had got trapped in a rabbit warren or badgers' sett.

Morgan decided not to scare them even more by mentioning the network of tunnels which the hill was rumoured to contain.

Cathy and Mike agreed to take one side of the hill and Morgan volunteered to take the other. As they parted company and Morgan was back in near silence she instinctively walked up to a patch covered by brambles. "Are you there Bruno?" she asked, and was rewarded by a whimpering noise. Clearing the area of undergrowth, she could see Bruno sat, apparently unhurt but undoubtedly very stuck, at the bottom of what may once have been either a tunnel or a Well, but which certainly went about six feet deep.

There was really only one option for it and checking nobody was watching her, she pointed at her feet and then at the bottom of the drop where Bruno sat patiently now and with her hands she pointed her extended fingers downwards to the spot where he sat as she floated slowly and feet first gently down to where Bruno was sitting.

He didn't look remotely surprised to be witnessing this and walked over to her licking first her feet and then her hand as she made a fuss of him while thrashing her legs happily with his tail.

"Come on then little pal, before your folks see how we're going to get out of here please," and with that she put her right arm around Bruno's waist and pointed her left arm straight upwards while looking skyward. Morgan and Bruno floated gently back to the safety of the hill where Morgan then blocked the hole in with a mass of bracken to prevent a similar incident happening to another dog.

She then turned to a now happy and relaxed, Bruno saying, "We'd better get you back to Cathy and Mike little boy." But as the words came out Cathy and Mike walked across the hill towards her and Bruno ran straight into an obviously very relieved Cathy's arms, looking back fixedly at Morgan just the once as though as to say 'thanks' to her.

A great happy ending now in place it was time to say her farewells to Cathy, Mike, and Bruno and to get back on the bus back home to her Mally.

As it pulled out she watched as Meon Hill decreased in size back into to the distance from the back window of the bus as Morgan planned to get back to her cat, her book and a nice large whisky and milk.

One day she would love to go flying over Meon Hill in person and take in all of its wonder and mystery, but for tonight she would do that in her dreams as she could always fly anywhere completely safely in her dreams and just enjoy the panoramic views and spectacle.

She retained the sight of the magical hill in her mind's eye so that when she nodded off the image would be vivid still and she could happily float around it from underneath her duvet.

Chapter Seven

Elouise Fernandez

It was 7.10pm at the Stage Door pub situated on The Strand in London. Half an hour ago Elouise and Ben had been rushed off their feet serving the pre-theatre clientele their drinks and food before they had all excitedly made their way on to whatever shows they were seeing that evening.

The place was now nearly silent, but the tables still needed clearing of the many glasses and plates which now lay abandoned on them.

Elouise quite liked tidying what looked like a bomb site as it took her mind away from thinking about what she should really be doing with her life.

She filled the glass washer with another cargo and returned another stack of plates to Marco in the kitchen and then stood outside the main door with her first cigarette in over two hours and watched the expectant theatregoers as they piled in to the many theatre entrances which she could clearly see without moving from where she stood. She made a mental note to change the water for the bluebells in the vases on the tables now the pub was unlikely to see much trade until the performances finished on or around 10.30pm.

She took a drag on her cigarette and watched as a young couple surveyed a large poster advertisement across the road for A View from the Bridge which was due to be staged next month, just around the corner at the Piccadilly Theatre.

Elouise loved that theatre and remembered her mother taking her there to see the opera musical 'Which Witch' at the beautiful theatre many years ago:

It had had wonderful songs and was set to thumping bass and was totally innovative, Elouise had sat transfixed through it and was in awe of the leading lady.

When she had returned home to Henley-In-Arden she had enrolled with the Beaudesert Players and had been cast in some decent roles and got great reviews in the local press, so it was a given that when her local collage introduced a performing arts course that she would enrol.

Her tutor Pauline had taken her under her wing and it was evident to everyone that she was the teacher's pet. It didn't matter to her fellow students as nobody else could match her acting and singing abilities.

Elouise's parents ran the Cowslip Inn and loved the place; it was a lovely black and white building with a creaky wooden floor and wooden chairs and tables with wonky legs but it was cosy and served wonderful food and local ale.

Every day Elouise's mother Flavia had put fresh bluebells out in vases on all of the tables and her father Juan would start the day by lighting the stove and baking bread while making them all porridge for breakfast. It was an idyllic family life and when she had shown such promise as an actress they had both been so proud of her.

It remained like that for many years and looking back Elouise wished she had realised just how lucky and happy she had been at the time.

Five years ago now Elouise's family life had changed irreparably and suddenly when Juan had been cooking a beef stroganoff in the kitchen and Elouise had been waiting the tables on the few customers they had in, when two police officers entered the Cowslip Inn and explained that Flavia had been in an accident and was in a critical condition at the hospital. Elouise had watched her father crumble before her and asked all the customers to leave immediately so they could both go and be with her at the hospital. She had even remembered to switch the cooker off.

In what seemed like a haze, it transpired Flavia, who neither of them had noticed pop out, had been crossing the road near the market place when a motorbike had ploughed straight into her meaning she fell awkwardly and landed heavily on her head causing a blood clot which was the cause of her critical condition. She had been holding a bunch of bluebells when she was hit.

Two days of sitting around miserably waiting for any news in the hospital followed until the life support machine was switched off and Juan and Elouise's lives seamed immediately to be less important.

Over the years father and daughter had remained close but it was as if the glue that held the family so tightly together had dissolved and Juan would just shut himself in the kitchen for hours at a time trying out new recipes.

It was also a jolt for Elouise who for years had lived an easy life with a guaranteed income from the inn, the kudos of appearing in many shows and the adoration of her loyal albeit only local fans.

Just over a year ago Elouise had moved to London to a tiny studio flat above an office in Wardour Street. It wasn't impressive but it was in central London and close to theatre land where it was her best opportunity to land a proper acting role on the west end stage.

She had since realised that anybody working in a pub in that area was harbouring a similar dream. Nobody moved to that part of London because they had a burning ambition to work behind a bar and fetch people sandwiches, no, they were all waiting for that one successful audition or for a theatre director to walk into the pub at the correct time and immediately spot their acting potential and star quality and hire them on the spot.

Elouise always read the Stage newspaper and had attended a few auditions over the past year as well as filming a couple of advertising commercials for stain remover and washing powder. It wasn't what she had envisaged but every time they were shown on the telly she received some royalties. It paid the bills, but what she wanted and her heart seemed to physically need was a role in a musical. She needed to tread the boards and sing to make her mother proud of her while breathing the same air as the audience and captivating people with what she could do, holding them enthralled by her every beautifully sung word.

There was a loud clatter of plates then followed by what was probably an Italian swearword emitting from the kitchen. Marco was picking up a pile of randomly shaped pieces of blue porcelain with a dustpan and brush as she approached.

"Do you want a hand Marco?" Elouise volunteered from the kitchen door. "I don't know why somebody can't organise a rota so that we have staff working here when we need them to be. Why let Claire wander off to her audition without putting someone else on duty?"

Elouise didn't have anything to do with the rota of course, she was just acting as Marco's sounding block and there would be even less point in saying there were no customers in the pub at the time when the plates would appear to have fallen, so she just smiled at him sympathetically.

What had got her back up though was her younger and prettier but squeakily voiced colleague Claire landing an audition when she hadn't been in the running for anything at all recently.

She knew on some level that her relatively new found emotions of jealously and loathing were at least in part due to her mother's untimely death and the falling apart of what had up until recently been a close relationship with her father. She also knew she was being irrational but she couldn't stop it.

About six months after Flavia had been killed she had walked into the kitchen of the Cowslip Inn to find her father and Michael, the rider of the motorbike which had killed her mother sitting together at the table drinking coffee and talking amicably.

Juan had got up and introduced her to Michael but Elouise couldn't even look him in the eye never mind have a conversation with him when he had tried to shake her hand, so she had simply turned her back on him and walked back out of the kitchen.

Her father later told her that Michael had been hugely upset by the events of the accident and was mortified and genuinely sorry about what he had done, he simply hadn't seen her mother there. It simply wasn't good enough for Elouise and never would be.

Juan accepting Michael's apology had seemed like a betrayal to Elouise, a lessening of her mother's worth and she and her father had argued about that constantly.

By now Elouise was just sorry she didn't get on with her old dad like she used to. She missed the Cowslip Inn, their soft lummox of a dog Bonzo and the sedate pace which things had moved at in the quiet market town.

Her mother was no longer around to constantly congratulate her on her achievements and buoy her up when things didn't go to plan and it felt like she was constantly side-lined for other artistes any time she tried to better herself, it was one blow of disappointment after another and certainly not for the want of trying on her part.

Claire had come back to work when everything was done and tidy and there was not a single customer in sight, all smiles and excitement about potentially being in the new production of Showboat.

Elouise could barely disguise her annoyance at the girl and so walked outside for another cigarette while Claire regaled the details of the audition to Ben who listened intently to her every word, not least because he fancied her and was quite possibly in love with her.

After breathing deeply while watching the pedestrians hasten up and down the Strand she went back into the pub and tried to avoid the cheery conversation interlaced with laughter as she replaced the water in the vases of bluebells on the tables. As she was the one sent out to get the flowers off the market each day they were always bluebells as a tribute to her mother.

When Elouise had finished Claire walked over to her with a big smile on her face and twinkling blue eyes. "You might as well knock off now Eli, I'll cover the after theatre trade if you like as you've been working all day."

Elouise smiled at the girl, which in itself proved what a good actress she was and picked up her handbag before walking the short distance home, stopping off just the once in the Dragon Inn for a large whisky with the intention of stopping her seething jealousy.

Of course it didn't work. Elouise tolerated her colleagues because she had to and she tolerated the customers so that she could afford to live, but she didn't much like any of them. She was not a team player and needed desperately to be a leading lady.

Elouise had spent two years at college studying for her degree in theatre and contemporary performance and she was determined to make good use of it.

She curled up in her tatty pink Dralon armchair having looked out of her window at the hustle and bustle of the activities of Soho in the street below her. Scantily clad women trying to snare smartly suited men to a backbeat of loud music and strobe lights. This street was full of smartly dressed and sombre office workers by day but the night time trade reeked of sex, money, and desperation and was infinitely louder.

Elouise tried to blank out the noise from the street as she concentrated on the jobs, castings, and auditions section of the Stage newspaper and concentrated on trying to find her big break into the theatres of London.

Every time she saw even a reference to a show which she had been in with the Beaudesert Players such as Godspell or Joseph with her mother gazing lovingly and proudly at her from the audience, all she could see was her mother's huge smile which was just for her. She had been a star in her community and all she had to do was do the same down here.

Among the umpteen cruise ship and holiday camp vacancies one stood out to her:

Director & Choreographer Nick Cameron will audition during June 2015:

'Dancers, Singers, Actors, and Graduates by invitation for TV, Theatre, West End & Commercial Representation. Email CV & photo to nickcameron.com.'

Elouise fired off yet another CV as well as a soft focus photograph and waited.

There were a number of adverts for parts in music videos and one requiring an elderly woman with a hearing aid for advertising work but also quite a few roles in a new production of the Doll's House by Ibsen were also being cast.

Elouise applied for both the part of Nora, wife to Torvald, friend to Rank and Christine, in debt to Krogstad and loving mother to her children. And also for the role of Christine, school friend to Nora and old flame of Krogstad. A warm, kind, and generous woman who gives attention rather than wanting to be the centre of it; she is unassuming whilst very perceptive, alert and aware of others.

Neither sounded anything like Elouise and both parts as well as the play seemed a bit dry, but it would be a start.

By now any half decent role was worth applying for as it would be a vast improvement on serving jacket potatoes to people who barely registered her existence.

She would kill for a part in one of the many big production glossy musicals in the west end, any part by now would do but she really ought to be the star. She had stunning looks, a wonderful voice, and could act her heart out. Why could nobody here see that?

She poured herself another whisky which bore no resemblance to a pub measure and walked over to the mirror for reassurance of her good looks.

She had long shiny brunette hair and flawless olive skin with soulful dark brown eyes framed with long dark lashes. She had inherited her mother's good looks and the combination of her mother's Argentinian heritage and her father's half-Greek, half Argentinian ancestry gave her a wonderful Latin-American look with beautiful features. Her full lips were coated in her trademark glossy pillar-box red lipstick. She had put on a couple of pounds since she had not danced for a while but nothing she couldn't shed easily.

Pouring the drink down her throat way too quickly she started to wallow at the injustice within her life.

Her laptop pinged and an e mail from Nick Cameron read, 'Sorry RADA or equivalent only. But good luck, Nick'.

Elouise was fuming. That was without knowing her from Adam and he must have spent less than five minutes going over her CV.

Sod it. She finished the remaining couple of inches of whisky left in the bottle and went to bed anticipating another day in the company of the squeaky and horribly cheerful Claire at the Stage Door the next day. Surely God had created her to do something more useful than this.

After a fitful sleep full of bouts of self-pity, she walked sluggishly to the Stage Door in good time for the pre-matinee trade.

Claire had got there before her and the first thing Elouise noticed was the pink carnations on the tables. Her incredulous glare must have spoken volumes as Claire breezily smiled at her. "I was here early and thought I'd get us some different flowers for a change, pretty aren't they?"

Elouise had never once explained the significance of the bluebells and the connection with her deceased mother so Claire had no chance at all of understanding what she had done wrong, but seeing Elouise's crestfallen expression she added, "I've got a new agent, a Nick Cameron, seems like a nice guy." Claire handed Elouise his business card as she walked back into the kitchen while saying over her shoulder with her customary smile, "You should call him, he seems good. Maybe he would represent you too."

This was the bloke who had turned her down last night and with whom Elouise was still livid about.

Claire walked back out of the kitchen with a tray of cutlery which she would polish before the lunchtime trade. "By the way, I got it! I'm part of the company for Showboat. How cool is that?"

"Well done," said Elouise grudgingly while trying to hold her simpering rage in check.

"Still, there will be plenty of extra shifts going begging here now," added Claire, which just enraged Elouise even more.

That was it. She walked outside of the door for a cigarette before she said something she would not be able to retract.

As she looked down amongst the cigarette butt ends she saw that a child must have dropped their water pistol there in the porch. It was a quite expensive looking pressurised one so when Elouise had calmed down slightly she took it back in with her and put it on top of her handbag. She didn't see an obvious use for it but it would be a shame to throw away something that would have cost someone a good few quid.

Ben was behind the bar now and as Elouise went to walk past him he said, "Your role is being cast for the Adelphi down the road you know." It was said affably; he was a nice lad.

It was no secret that Elouise's dream role was that of Evita. Her Argentinian heritage, her strength of voice, and her looks were just perfect for the role and she absolutely loved the songs and the power within them.

"I take it you mean Evita?" Ben pulled his latest 'Actors Circle' magazine from under the bar counter and showed her the advert which he had circled for her.

Trembling as she wrote down the phone number she gave him a peck on the cheek. "Thanks for thinking of me," and then, with steely eyes which Eva Peron herself would have been proud of, she said forcefully, "I have got to get that part."

Chapter Eight

A Film Review

Morgan was absolutely elated when she got into work. She knew she ought to have at least some sympathy for the arts correspondent Sammy, but she had put that to the back of her mind as for today at least she was going to be doing one of her dream jobs.

It was very rare for Morgan to have a proper conversation with Juliet Moore the Editor of the Stratford Chronicle, but today she had been invited into her office for a chat. It was like finally making it into the inner sanctum. Morgan had made it clear to anybody who would listen for a very long time that she would like to review the films and plays for the Chronicle and since Sammy had had an unfortunate misunderstanding with her horse Pandora, resulting in her landing awkwardly on the deck on a country lane and breaking her right wrist into the bargain, it looked like Morgan had finally got her big chance.

She couldn't help smiling as Juliet regaled the details of Sammy's riding accident and she was wondering to herself how long a broken wrist would take to heal as unfortunately Sammy was right handed and so writing out her reviews would be out of the question at the moment. She them briefly chastised herself for being so opportunist.

Juliet made it absolutely clear that this would be a temporary arrangement to help them out of a hole until either Sammy could return to work or a freelancer could be taken on and it was also made abundantly clear that Morgan would have to keep her hand in with the sales department as she was the papers best-selling saleswoman.

Still, although it had been handed to her very begrudgingly when she had left Juliet's office she had still got the job she aspired to have, even if it was unknown to all how long for.

She beamed at Rose as she walked past her and checked how Mally was doing in the mirror while putting her coat on, and having watched Mally happily snoozing in a patch of sunshine by the window she took herself out into the cool air and practically skipped to the cinema with a huge grin on her face.

Sammy was supposed to attend the matinee and press preview of Pressure today and file her review the following day, so in her place Morgan rocked up and bought a large tub of popcorn and a medium Fanta from Paul who congratulated her on her new position and went to take her seat in the nearly empty cinema where she took out her large notebook and favourite cartridge pen and placed them on the seat next to hers ready for when she had any moments of inspiration to impart to the pad.

Juliet had told her to look beyond the story being told and while he served her popcorn Paul had suggested she concentrate on the jealousy and fear of failure that ran throughout the film, but it would be Morgan's words that counted in the end as she sat back in her comfy reclining seat and took a large swig of Fanta.

She noted the director's name as the opening titles rolled and those of the leading cast members and settled back to enjoy the film while thinking about how best to critique it.

The screen was filled with the beautiful face of Colin Radcliffe and Morgan couldn't believe she was being paid to watch the stunning man.

The film opened in Serbia where a warlord was seemingly calling all the shots, until Colin's character Robert Vine had been hired to bring him and his despicable regime down.

There were many issues surrounding immigration and Morgan made a note to elaborate on that as well as the overriding sense of fear, not of each other's characters but of their own failings as human beings due to their oppression.

There were guns being threatened to be used throughout the film, but very few shots were made as the guns were props for the weak people to hide themselves behind and Morgan scribbled a note to herself to the effect that the strong people and those who were comfortable in their own skin in the film were the same ones that didn't need to carry any weapons.

There was an odd parochial element to the film whereby nobody from outside of Serbia was held in any level of respect and certainly didn't deserve to be listened to, or acknowledged, and Morgan made a note to herself about what she was seeing played out before her in this regard.

She also noted the lack of females cast in the film which could reasonably infer that all the big huge problems that exist in the world must be solved by assertive men.

There was a section of the film which concentrated on war crimes and since Morgan knew nothing about the history of Serbia and whether this was true or not she wrote a note to herself to either ignore that bit completely or read something about Serbian history between now and tomorrow morning.

Robert Vine was the hero of the film and after various men got shot he was left to pick up the pieces and reallocate stolen money and possessions back to their rightful owners as well as protect and reassure local families who lived in constant fear for their own lives as well as those of their families in a country seemingly constantly at war.

Morgan wrote a note to herself to write about the effects of war on the family units.

Filling her mouth with popcorn she concentrated on the beautiful actor before her and mused about the one-upmanship running throughout the film and how, in a war time culture, it manifested itself into having more possessions than others, or as in this film, instilling the most fear in other people.

That was it, she thought, she could write about the capitalist elements and the need to rule others by fear.

She would omit the actual ending from her review as well as the fact that unfortunately the film although pretty good with lots of things to think about regarding human nature had ultimately descended into a love story between Robert Vine and one of the Serbian women who he had rescued from oppression. That was a waste of a strong story to make it ultimately about romance. Surely somebody should have shown a bit more creativity than that and surely the woman would have more pressing things on her mind than hooking up with a man.

The end titles rolled and good had prevailed over evil and the good guy had won the pretty girl. Oh dear, she would have to concentrate on jealousy and fear as themes running through her review.

As she went to get up a smell of lavender filled the auditorium and as she looked back at the screen a large image of Snowbell the Samoyed appeared on the screen looking out at her as though pleading with his eyes to Morgan not to forget him or his family. Morgan had not forgotten about him at all though, she just needed to know more about what she was supposed to be doing to help them.

The intensity with which she had been watching the film and forming words to describe it had blotted out the imposed images that formed a considerable part of her everyday life, but she was sure that when she got home they would be back and would hopefully make more sense sometime soon.

Still, she absolutely must do a good job of writing up her film review this evening as she had to impress Juliet and keep this job for a while longer at least. It was just a shame the ending of the film had been so anticlimactic and dull when the events and motivations in the story were interesting and should have been better explored.

Leaving the auditorium, she held the door open for a smartly dressed gentleman in a dapper navy blue suit. He was aged around sixty and pleasant looking with white hair and twinkly azure blue eyes, but was walking with a slight limp. "Did you enjoy the film?" asked Morgan and when their eyes connected she could feel his disappointment.

"I wrote the book it was based on," the man nodded. "It was supposed to be about the waste and the bewilderment that became the norm for many years in Serbia."

Morgan asked his name and if she could quote him on that for the Chronicle. James Gazi was happy to be quoted and even offered to have a chat with Morgan about what he wrote originally, before tinsel town had completely changed the focus. They shared a pot of earl grey tea together in the quiet cinema bar and Mr Gazi regaled his experiences in Serbia as part of a protection team and what he had endeavoured to achieve to help people who could no longer afford to trust others and to promote peace when all the people of the country had known for many years was fighting.

James Gazi had spent many years living out in Belgrade and he joked that the reason for his limp was that a bullet had moved a lot quicker than him when he was trying to get out of its way.

He explained about Territories of the Republic of Bosnia and Herzegovina and the Republic of Croatia which was controlled by the Bosnian and Croatian Serb forces, after Operation Corridor in July 1992.

Serbia was involved in the Yugoslav Wars in the period between 1991 and 1999 – the war in Slovenia, the war in Croatia, the war in Bosnia, and the war in Kosovo. During this period, Slobodan Milosevic was the authoritarian leader of Serbia, which was in turn part of the Federal Republic of Yugoslavia. "So many wars – Too many wars," he said reflectively, but then gave her a gentle smile.

He was not only an intelligent and knowledgeable man but also rather jocular as he joked that he was going to have to wander home to show his cat a good dad in the near future.

Looking behind Mr Gazi, at the Monet print of water lilies which was hanging on the wall behind him, she could see a rather overweight but beautifully coloured stripy ginger cat with bright green eyes looking intently at them from inside the glass which was surrounded by a scrubbed pine frame.

Morgan took out her notepad and wrote down some notes on the wars and thanked Mr Gazi profusely for the insight he had given her. She pledged to read his book which the film was based on. It was called 'The last thing left in Pandora's box' as the only thing he had to give over the decade of the conflict was hope.

Mr Gazi politely stood up when Morgan did and as he gently smiled at her and his brilliant blue eyes twinkled the kindness and sincerity came off him in waves. "Lovely to meet you Morgan but my pal Boris will be requiring his catering staff by now." He was a thoroughly lovely man, thought Morgan, and she hoped they would meet again one day.

She walked home with her notes and her many ideas for the film review and as she walked into the hall of her house she watched a lone robin looking out at her from the mirror which hung there.

Mally opened one eye in a welcoming gesture and after climbing down from the settee he padded softly around her legs before walking her to the kitchen to fetch his chicken tea and a saucer of milk.

While he was safely tucking in to his feast Morgan got out her laptop computer and began typing up her review of 'Pressure'. The plot was flimsy, but with James Gazi's insight into what the story should have been about she managed to paint a picture of what life during the Balkan conflicts was really like and she hoped that he would have approved.

As he was such a nice man she even gave his book a plug as well as mentioning just how dishy Colin Radcliffe was in the role that he had created. She didn't even bother mentioning about him getting the girl in the end, that was just boring.

After reading through the review numerous times and changing many of the words around she decided she had created a review she was happy with and so turned on the telly to watch the evening news.

It was the commercial break and a rather exotic looking woman with sad eyes that didn't go with her beaming smile was trying to sell her washing powder. It was odd, but for some reason while watching the woman do her best attempt at selling her cleaning products she could envisage the image of the pressurised water pistol which had made no sense to her the other day and made even less sense in this context.

She took her boots off and snuggled down on the settee with Mally who had just landed on her to watch the news. It was all about the forthcoming general election and Morgan took some interest in it, but nobody was promising anything that would affect her life or Mally's in any way they would notice particularly.

All seemed quiet except for the arguments and fighting on the telly as she watched the soap operas and then a reasonable instalment of a new drama starring David Tennant but unfortunately she had guessed how it was going to end a long way out even before the image of the lovely Snowbell came to the fore of the screen blocking out what was happening in the background.

She poured herself a whisky and milk and gazed back at the beautiful dog. "It's no good Snowbell, you or somebody is going to have to show me what all this is about if you want me to help."

With that the image of the dog faded to be replaced by the end credits of the drama.

Morgan poured herself another whisky and milk and stood watching the stars while drinking it, she was rather proud of her day's work.

She and Mally then went to bed and he snuggled against her shoulder purring happily as they both nodded off.

At around two in the morning Morgan found herself floating just above the bed. but felt a sense of calmness as she looked down on the sleeping figures of herself and Mally below her so she simply relaxed and went back to sleep and the dream she was having where Mally was making friends and having his own adventures with Boris the ginger cat. It looked like they were having great fun playing contentedly with each other.

She awoke early in the morning as sunshine was streaming through the window and onto a patch of the duvet where Mally had curled up in it, obviously basking in the warmth and light.

After a bowl of cereal and a large mug of strong coffee Morgan gave her faithful friend a stroke and an extra bowl of biscuits to tide him through until she returned from work, and checking all was calm in her hall mirror she left to show off her work to Juliet at the Chronicle.

She said good morning to Rose and walked past her to hang her coat up while checking Mally was safely tucked up at home. He had found the one patch of sunshine which had reached the arm of the settee and was happily sunbathing on that spot even though it looked like a most uncomfortable and precarious position.

Rose said something without moving from her desk while perusing Morgan quizzically, "Whenever you look into that mirror you smile you know, is that a form of narcissism or what?"

Before Morgan had thought of a suitable response Juliet's door swung open and the elegantly be suited editor invited her in to her office. "I thought I could hear voices," she smiled. "How did you get on with the film review?"

Suppressing an urge to grin Morgan handed her review across the desk for Juliet's perusal and casually pointed out that she had met and interviewed the author who had written the book which the film was based on and had included what the meaning of the film was supposed to be alongside assessing the Hollywood version of the tale.

Juliet raised an eyebrow while still reading the review. After what was possibly five minutes or so, but felt like an age, Juliet looked up from the paper and declared, "I'm very impressed, based on this quality of work you can go and review Death of a Salesman next week." Morgan pondered about joking that she was unlikely to procure an interview with Arthur Miller while she was at it but decided to keep the thought to herself and just enjoy knowing she was in her new role for at least another week. It didn't pay anything like as much as the commission that the advertising sales had reaped for her but so what, she and Mally could afford to eat and this was much more fun than looking across the office at Rose's glowering face.

She hoped this would turn into a more permanent job one day, but she already knew really in her heart that it would. She had faith and there was no hurry.

Chapter Nine

Ted Clarke

Ted Clarke was walking with difficulty down Brick Lane in London and nobody was taking any notice of him whatsoever. Even though the pavement was crowded with people, he was invisible.

This was his most pleasurable part of the day. He was away from his grim and dusty little flat in the grotty part of Westminster that was Tower Hamlets and he at least had a little bit of hope that one of his horses would come in for him. He was on his way to the bookies to split a fiver between the ten horses he had trawled over the form of in the daily newspaper earlier and was going to spend the afternoon watching the racing in the bookies with each of the horses carrying his 50p to win bet. Right now he still had the hope that they would all come in. That was as much hope as his life contained these days.

It was starting to rain and his arthritis was giving him jip so he arrived at 'GH Ruff Turf Accountant' just as he needed a sit down. He landed none to gracefully on a stool and took his notes out from his pocket transferring his list of potential winners to ten individual betting slips and then walked slowly over to the counter where the fragrant Tracy took his bets with a slight but unconvincing smile. As she put the bets into the system Ted looked around to see a couple of old boys watching the racing channel on the TV in the corner, but no other sign of life. That was fine by him. He loved watching the gorgeous horses but was much less keen on spending time with people.

He pottered around the betting office between races talking to nobody but reading the form on the Racing Post pages which were attached to the cork boards on the walls with drawing pins.

Of his ten runners, five were at the back of the field, one was third, two were second and two were winners: Skyrocket had come in for him by two lengths at $10 - 1$ and Minerva had come in ten lengths ahead at $6 - 1$. Far more importantly to him all the horses had come home safely.

Ted decided his profit could buy him a sandwich and a pint at the 'Old Nag' pub just up the road.

As he left the bookies in silence he waddled up the road to the pub, his huge frame exasperating his difficulty in walking without being in pain and as he walked into the pub nobody registered his existence.

Years ago when he had walked into this same pub with Richard people would turn around and greet them in a friendly manner, but they had always been Richard's friends really and had all slowly taken flight when he had become ill to the extent that not one person in this area was now even his acquaintance let alone his friend.

He used to have exotic tastes and had loved sampling the Bengali cuisine in the many restaurants in and around Brick Lane when he had first arrived to London, but now he was quite happy to blend into the background and pretend he didn't exist while eating his cheese and pickle sandwich and enjoying his pint of Bass.

It had all been so very different when he and Richard had first moved to London. They were in awe of the bright lights and multitude of things to do in a thriving city centre. It had been so very different and exciting compared to their upbringing in the sedate but pretty Glastonbury in Somerset.

Twenty-five years ago it had been Richard that had persuaded him to move to this area. They were both builders by trade and there was no shortage of gainful employment for those willing to work so largely if not completely because of Richard's infectious enthusiasm they had moved to the tiny third floor flat which Ted now lived his miserable existence alone.

It had been great at first: trying new foods and watching exotic people of different colours and creeds going about their daily business. He had missed the tranquillity and mystique of Glastonbury where he had looked across at the Tor lovingly every morning when he woke and where he would often visit the Chalice Well to listen to the water gently trickling and to enjoy the peace and serenity of the idyllic garden it was incorporated into. But then Richard Hart crashed into his sedate but contented life, and made him fall in love with him and then died a long and painful death which Ted could only stand by and observe while making platitudes and reiterating his undying love.

Richard had contracted HIV just before they had met and embarked on their whirlwind romance and resultant mutual love and partnership. He was always the lively party person, the cheerful guy that everybody had liked and Ted had never got over Richard's untimely and unnecessary death, which was caused by Kaposi's sarcoma which had caused a tumour of the blood vessel walls. The cancer is apparently rare in people not infected with HIV, but common in HIV-positive people and Richard had left him so quickly, too quickly, for Ted to say and do all he had wanted to. There were so many things they had left to do, shows and films to see, and books to read and discuss together.

Kaposi's sarcoma usually appears as pink, red or purple lesions on the skin and mouth. In people with darker skin such as Richard's lovely olive skin, the lesions can look dark brown or even black. Kaposi's sarcoma can also affect the internal organs, including the digestive tract and lungs and Richard's lungs had simply given out on him.

Richard had not only been a live-wire with a permanent smile on his face, he was also so disarmingly stunning with his glossy black hair and tanned olive skin from working outside, but towards the end he had looked gaunt and blotchy with sunken eyes and it was as though the life was slowly being sucked out of him. His wonderful shiny, clever, and funny soulmate looked decidedly lack-lustre.

Ted alternated from blaming Richard himself for dying and leaving him, God for being so spiteful in taking him away, and the council for being as much use as chocolate teapots in their hour of need. The council usually got his vitriol because they were the easiest to attack.

On his bookshelves at his home there were more box files containing correspondence to and from the council than there were books by now. They were covered in a layer of dust as Ted wasn't any great fan of housework.

Over the years he had complained about so many things in his council flat that he was on first name terms with many of the staff.

He had complained the boiler didn't work, there was damp coming through the ceiling, the leaves were falling onto the pavement creating a health and safety hazard and the lift didn't work most of the time. He didn't want to use the lift as it alternated between being used as a toilet or for the local teenagers to have sex in but that wasn't the point.

The constant battle with the council was an outlet for his grief and a distraction from looking at the utter waste his life had become.

His latest crusade was to try to get rehomed as the stairs were too sharp for him to climb with his arthritis and the lift was constantly out of order. It did not cross his mind that his obesity might be playing a part with regard to this. Ted had even roped in his local MP Grant Ruffelle who had not responded to the last two letters he had written to him and the response from him from his initial letter was just a bland, 'Thank you for bringing the matter to my attention'. That had really made his blood boil.

Ted was pondering his next move while taking his time eating his sandwich when he was disturbed from his musing by a smartly suited man carrying a glass of orange juice and a cheese cob asking if he could sit with him.

The pub was filling up and there were no other tables free so Ted agreed. The odd thing was the man had kept eye contact with him and asked for his agreement. In his experience of London people usually just did what they wanted without even the slightest consultation.

"Is this your local?" broached Roy Spencer after he had sat down opposite Ted, having placed his orange juice down and taken a couple of bites out of his cheese cob.

"I don't dine out often any more, but I had a couple of horses come in for me and they bought me my lunch today," said Ted honestly.

Roy smiled and replied, "I haven't looked at the horses in years, maybe I will now I've got more time now."

It was said more to himself than to Ted. He had to find a purpose and a worthwhile use for his time soon that brought in some money before his wife found out what he had been up to and how he had lost his job. He couldn't just keep wandering around London avoiding Maxine and pretending to go out to work each morning. It was a thought.

Across the table from him Ted was pondering the last time he had dined out with anyone, or even had a proper conversation with someone.

When he and Richard had first moved to London they had embraced the multi-cultural atmosphere around the East End and had sampled many of the traditional English pie and mash delights as well as embracing the Bengali cuisine and culture.

Richard had always easily made friends with the waiters, waitresses and barmaids they had encountered and had enjoyed learning about their different backgrounds.

Ted smiled faintly as he remembered Richard bursting into their flat one day holding a Piper Chaba and excitedly retelling its relevance as newly learnt from the girl on the market stall where he had bought it:

In Bangladesh apparently, the stems of the plant are used as a spice in meat and fish dishes. In most countries of South and South-East Asia, the fruit of the Piperaceae vines is well known as a spice and is called the 'long pepper'. However, in Bangladesh the use of Choi Jhal is unique, because the twigs, stems or roots of Piper Chaba, not the fruit, are used as a spice. It is a relatively expensive spice in Bangladesh, and the roots are usually more expensive than the stems because of their stronger aroma. The taste is similar to horseradish or so Simla had told him.

Neither Richard nor Ted had ever tried to eat the thing and even today it was still sitting on the kitchen windowsill gathering dust, but prompting fond memories whenever Ted looked at it.

They had both loved animals and were both vegetarians and they loved nothing more than to frequent the Taj Mahal Restaurant run by Ambi just around the corner from the docklands and eat a leisurely pointed gourd curry together, while drinking Indian beer and making a big fuss of Ambi's gorgeous black chow chow dog, Mowgli.

That was the only problem with the pokey flat. They would both have loved to have had a dog.

They had both loved learning new things about different cultures and foods and Ambi had been happy to sit down with them and explain what a pointed gourd actually was. They had both listened intently as he had said that colloquially, in India, it is often called a green potato. It is widely cultivated in the eastern part of India, particularly in Orissa, Bengal, Assam, Bihar, and Uttar

Pradesh. It is a vine plant, similar to cucumber and squash, though unlike those it is perennial.

They had both looked down at their plates then after Ambi had finished telling his tale and laughed as both were almost too afraid to eat something so interesting. They even read what each other was thinking at that moment. It was lovely to remember that laughing and shared thought of not wanting to touch the green potato and he smiled at the memory.

Mistaking Ted's smile for friendliness towards him and breaking Ted's thoughts which he was enjoying so much Roy asked, "Well if you've backed a couple of winners do you have any good tips for later his afternoon?"

Ted decided this man was okay and suggested Stately Pride in the 3.40pm at Kempton. "He is a course and distance winner there but hasn't run for a while now so should go off at a good price."

Now having an excuse for something to do Roy finished his cob and his orange juice and bade Ted farewell with a smile. "If it comes in I'll buy you a pint or two," Roy said leaving the table and making his was slowly to the bookies.

Ted thought no more of the meeting and polished off his sandwich and pint before making his way slowly back to the flat in Tower Hamlets.

As he walked up the bustling pavements it was as though he had become invisible again, but his arthritis felt a bit better and as he dawdled past the many restaurants he again remembered the laughter and good food he had once shared with his soul mate behind their doors. They had been wonderful times.

He looked at the view across to the docklands and pondered just how much the place had changed since he and Richard had first moved to the area.

Then it had been easy to find work on a building site, as a labourer if necessary, but there had always been work if you were willing to do it.

There was nothing for a manual worker around here anymore.

Now it was all office work and finance or computers and if he was looking for a job today he wouldn't know where to start. It was academic really as he was now too fat and arthritic to go anywhere near a building site and certainly wouldn't get hired to do anything useful anytime soon.

He channelled his energies into complaining about his existence now. Too miserable to even contemplate a different life for himself and certainly never involving another relationship. No. that was it now, he would eat, drink. Back horses, reminisce about what was and decide who to target at the council with his next pointless battle.

He just hoped when he died he would be with Richard again. It was something for him to look forward to.

As he approached the dingy tower block that contained his pokey flat which sunlight seemed to avoid, he noticed a group of youths drinking lager out of cans and swearing and so as he had done so often before he lowered his head and walked deliberately t but painfully up the stairs to his tiny empire. There was just one yell of "Fat Git," directed at his back today, so that was an improvement on the usual raft of worse insults.

He sat on his worn out and threadbare grey velour settee with its worn out springs recovering from his walking and waiting for his heavy breathing to return to normal when he noticed the letter he had received from Grant Ruffelle was still sitting on his glass coffee table. He would think carefully about his next strategy as he was not going to be fobbed off or ignored by that Tory toff anymore. His latest mission was to get rehomed. This was nothing to do with the steep stairs or the dodgy lift if truth be told. It was because this was the very flat which Richard had died in and Ted could still remember seeing him lying in their bed cold and lifeless with rigamortis already setting in but his eyes still looking across at him, by the time Ted had woken up, turned around and realised his lover had left him. Ted had been asleep and hadn't said goodbye properly. The guilt was with him whenever he entered that bedroom and tears were never far from his eyes when he remembered that sight.

The flat was silent but for the loud thoughts going around Ted's mind.

Chapter Ten

Boris the Cat

Morgan looked in the hall mirror as she was on her way in from work and saw the handsome ginger cat which she knew to be Boris: Friend to James Gazi.

He looked totally content and instead of Morgan feeling she needed to keep an eye on him she got the distinct impression that Boris was keeping tabs on her.

Mally was up and waiting for his tea and she pointed out to him that he was always her number one boy.

Having fed him and stoked his head she switched the telly on and saw it was an advert for Snow Dust washing powder. It was that exotic looking girl again, but as she made eye contact through the screen with the beautiful woman she could see there was something not at all right about the woman.

Looking into her lovely but cold eyes she picked up on hatred and an obsession emitting from the otherwise gorgeous woman. It wasn't just disappointment or a bad day it was as if these emotions were what was driving her very existence.

As she looked away from the screen she noticed Mally sitting by the front window watching something quizzically. As she went over to look at what the subject of fascination was she saw that Boris was sitting bolt upright in the centre of the lawn gazing back at them as if he owned the place.

As she patted Mally on the head and walked out into the garden to have a chat with him he just continued to sit there and look alternately from Mally to Morgan and back again.

Morgan got the impression that Boris was James's familiar as Mally was hers.

They both seemed to be very attune to their respective humans if not more attune than both humans were.

The witch's familiar is a constant companion of a witch, they are drawn together as if by a magnet, each intuitively knowing they are meant to be together, they are similar in character as both witch and cat are astute, wise, and independent. When the witch and cat are at work together the magic pull is extremely powerful and they know instinctively that it is meant to be, a bonding takes place and the two form a lifelong alliance. Cats have a mysterious air about them and have for centuries been linked to all matters occult.

Boris gracefully walked past Morgan and into the house where he casually padded over to Mally and nuzzled him whilst giving his ears a wash.

To her astonishment Mally then rolled on to his back and gently pawed Boris's nose.

They would appear to have become firm friends instantly.

Not only was it lovely to have Boris as a guest but Morgan couldn't help but think it would give her an ideal opportunity to meet up with James again in the not too distant future. She had thoroughly enjoyed their brief time together and looked forward to the prospect of catching up with him again.

Mally and Boris were now settled while gazing out of the window together and indulging in a spot of joint bird watching. Boris had the loveliest bright green eyes and judging by his lovely glossy coat was no doubt pampered and groomed by James every day.

Presuming he was staying for high tea Morgan got them both a bag of treats to share from the kitchen although it certainly didn't look like Boris needed building up.

As she glanced at the telly as she was passing she paid vague attention to a party political broadcast as it was coming up to an election but far more attention to the group of robins which had formed in front of the leader of the Liberal Democrats which were happily singing away. Fortunately, the lure of the treats meant neither of her furry friends could be bothered to register them, let alone consider trying to do anything about them.

After an hour watching the soap operas Morgan looked across to see Mally and Boris cuddled together snoozing happily by the window with their paws wrapped around each other. They had slept through the yelling of a romantic break up as well as a nasty car crash on the telly, but comfy and sweet though they looked together Morgan decided she had better get Boris home in case James was worried about him.

As she walked across and stroked both cats on the head she explained to Mally that she had better get his new friend safely home and he purred at her knowingly.

Boris got up, yawned, and walked casually across to the front door while Morgan picked up her keys from the bowl in the hall. She checked the mirror on her way out and saw a bunch or bluebells as well as a bunch of lavender. Whatever it meant it was certainly very pretty.

As she opened the front door Boris stepped out and looked around at her as if instructing her to follow him. As the top of her road they turned right and when they were halfway up the road Boris sat and looked both ways before padding across the road with Morgan by his side across to a smart bungalow with a beautifully manicured front garden which Boris plonked himself down on pointedly.

"Really Boris, this is your home is it? You and James live just around the corner from us do you?" and as she bent down to give him a pat on the head she heard the front door open and a casually dressed James Gazi beamed at them showing his lovely white teeth.

"You've collected our new friend then have you boy?" without a hint of surprise in his voice. "I was just about to get myself a drink if you'd like to join me in one," suggested James, and Boris wandered into his home with Morgan following behind him. "Whisky and milk for you is it my dear?"

That was odd as it was an unusual drink of choice and she had only drunk tea with James on their first meeting, but she nodded and smiled at him while he gestured for her to take a seat in the armchair in the living room. As she sat and admired the sumptuous surroundings and huge collection of books James had amassed Boris sat on the arm of her red velour armchair which she noticed was covered in fur as this was obviously his usual spot.

James handed Morgan a lovely crystal tumbler containing a very generously sized whisky and milk and sat down on the red sofa in front of his huge bookcase which was packed with hardbacks to face her with a large glass of red wine in his hand. "I do like a nice glass of wine around this time of day," and he raised his glass as if as a toast to her.

His silver grey hair shone a bright white in the sunlight and Morgan asked if he had done something different with it. "Had my ears lowered yesterday," said James with a smile that enhanced his sculptured high cheek bones, "you like it?" Morgan hadn't thought this man to be so good looking when they last met, it had been how interesting his life was that had appealed to her, but now she saw him in a different light and blushed and nodded in answer to his question.

"So, how did the film review go down?" broached James from in front of what was a large amount of books about politics and political leaders including Hitler and Stalin.

"Very well with my Boss thanks, I seem to have done alright as I'm reviewing 'Death of a Salesman' next."

"Ah, Arthur Miller, I prefer 'The Crucible', but I'm sure I've got a copy of 'Salesman' if you'd like to borrow it."

"Great," smiled Morgan. "I gather it's all about the American Dream."

James explained that the 'American Dream' is indeed the theme of the play, but everyone in the play has their own way to describe their own American dreams.

Throughout the play the lead character Willy Loman has flashbacks and it is found that he believes success is indicated through someone who is rich, well liked, and demonstrates a good personality. He believes that someone who is rich and well-liked is being successful and that raises many other issues and questions about what success actually is.

"Tell you what my dear, I'll dig out the book for you and get us some cheese and biscuits. I'm a little bit peckish are you?"

When he left the room she gave Boris a stroke while admiring further her surroundings. On the wall behind her was a large and beautiful painting of the Egyptian Cat Goddess Bastet in a golden frame, and next to that on the wall was a lovely mahogany framed clock which she noticed looking at her watch was seven minutes fast. As she looked at the golden carriage clock with its rotating pendulum which was taking pride of place on the windowsill she noticed that too was also set seven minutes fast.

James came back into the room and set a china plate with a large lump of crumbly cheddar and some crackers down on the coffee table which got the attention of Boris as he sat up and pricked his ears. He then popped into his study with its oak panelled library which was again full of books but on pretty much any subject imaginable and walked straight up to the shelf containing his set of Arthur Miller's plays and returned to his seat opposite Morgan after handing the book across to her for which she thanked him and turned it over to read the blurb on the play.

"Lovely picture of Bastet," declared Morgan after putting the book to one side while James cut the cheese and placed it on the crackers and beckoned her to help herself. He then picked up a small morsel of cheese and placed in on the arm of the chair in front of Boris and ruffled his cat's ears while Boris tucked in appreciatively.

"Ah yes the lovely Bastet. We obviously share a love of cats. It makes far more sense to me to worship a cat than anything in any other form."

"I couldn't agree more, they are so much lovelier and brighter than people," nodded Morgan while speaking with her mouth full of cheese.

"Bastet was also known as the Goddess of Perfumes you know," said James as an aside as he helped himself to a cracker and put another morsel of cheese on the chair arm for Boris.

"Your Boris seems to be as well looked after as my Mally," said Morgan as she watched the pair of them fondly.

"A house is not a home without a cat. And my Boris is a rather special cat," James said while patting him on the head.

"The two of you live alone then?" broached Morgan, casually she hoped.

"I've never wanted to live with another human being and I was never that fussed about girls. I've got everything I want in life here now. Nice house, nice life and a lovely cat. That's all I need."

Morgan was rather impressed with his answer as she had always thought much the same way about her own lifestyle. It was nice to find a kindred spirit.

She helped herself to another cracker and took what she hoped was a ladylike sip of her whisky and milk while admiring the lovely living room. There was a huge bunch of pink carnations on the far windowsill which were arranged to perfection.

Looking across the spines of the books in front of her she asked, "Is it the people or the politics you are interested in with Hitler and the like?"

James pondered the question for a moment.

"I'm not that keen on people as a species and don't have a huge amount of time for them, but I do wonder what drives them and it's really rather worrying how individuals have shaped history to the detriment of the environment. A lot of people could do with being protected from themselves never mind leading weaker people to join in and agree with them and their dangerous ideas."

Again Morgan couldn't agree more. She wasn't about to explain her more peculiar traits, but she did spend a fair amount of time protecting people from themselves when in truth she would much rather settle down at home with Mally.

She was enjoying herself hugely but knew she would be happy to get back home to her own furry friend in due course.

Remembering the General Election was going ahead and helping herself to another cracker Morgan broached, "I watched the Lib Dem broadcast before coming here, they seem the best of a bad bunch."

James said that in his time he had stood to become both a Labour and a Conservative Councillor but had failed on both counts. "I just hope Nigel Farage doesn't get any power, he's like Hitler but without the charm, intelligence, or talent."

Morgan chuckled.

"Really. At least Hitler loved his dogs and he was a talented artist. If the Austrians had let him study art there the course of history might have been very different."

Morgan loved both art and dogs so could easily warm to that argument.

"What we really take for granted in this country is the choices we can make. Milosevic's government exercised influence and censorship in the media. An example was in March 1991, when Serbia's Public Prosecutor ordered a 36-hour blackout of two independent media stations, B92 Radio and Studio B television to prevent the broadcast of a demonstration against the Serbian government taking place in Belgrade. Over here we have free speech and many choices but we still rarely learn from history."

They polished off the last of the cheese between them and James put the plate on the floor so that Boris could jump down and eat all the crumbs which didn't take him long at all.

"I'm yet to be convinced why people think they are superior to other animals never mind each other," broached Morgan.

"That is a very reasonable statement my dear," smiled James while taking a sip of his wine.

It was a lovely interesting evening and after discussing media and politics further including how Che Guevara was instrumental in creating the clandestine radio station Radio Rebelde, or Rebel Radio, in February 1958 which broadcast news to the Cuban people with statements by the 26th of July movement, and provided radio telephone communication between the growing number of rebel columns across the island over her second large whisky and milk while James had another red wine. She decided while looking across at the now snoozing Boris that it must be time to go home to her Mally.

She got up a little unsteadily and thanked James for an interesting evening. "I'm sure we'll meet again in the near future," said James while hugging her in a gesture of farewell.

She gently stoked Boris as he slept and James escorted her to the front door and bade her good evening while handing her the Arthur Miller book. He was still waving to her as she walked across the road on her way home. As she looked back from a little further down the road she saw that he had now closed the door but two hedgehogs looked to be having a conversation on his front lawn. It was rather idyllic and they seemed to know they were perfectly safe while chatting there.

Happily strolling back home she put the key in the door which woke Mally up and he ambled over to the hall to greet her. "I've just spent a lovely evening with your friend Boris and his dad," she explained while bending down to stroke him. "They are two very lovely people," and Mally purred as if hanging on to and agreeing with her every word.

She looked in her hall mirror and saw James's clock reflected back at her. She checked her watch and saw that it was still precisely seven minutes fast. She smiled to herself and was most perturbed when the image gently faded away to be replaced with an image of an overweight man she had met but who seemed to exude anger and a sense of injustice from every pore. Whatever he wanted from her she felt no inclination to help him as she could sense that whatever his problem was it was completely self-inflicted.

She looked away and walked across the lounge to switch the telly on. The image on the screen was of the exotic looking girl in the washing powder advert with the unsmiling eyes. The picture was unmoving and had frozen so she switched the set top box on and off and rather oddly the commercial came back to life and was played out in full from start to finish. Was somebody really trying to tell her that she needed to buy some washing powder?

She settled down on the settee with Mally. She had had quite enough whisky and milk for one day so settled for a snooze with her friend curled up on her stomach pawing at her gently.

They settled down and watched a documentary about the Egyptian Cat Goddess Bastet while snuggled up together. It was odd how many times a recent conversation or thought was played out in full with its lengthier meaning explained not long after the original reference.

They were a funny lot the Egyptians as over the course of history they had gone from killing cats to revering them under the banner of religion she learnt.

It was a rather fascinating programme and only interrupted by some loud purring from just above her stomach and the occasional floating sprig of lavender and the odd bluebell floating across the screen in front of the iconic images of Bastet.

As they finished their viewing together and the end credits rolled Morgan thought she saw a pink carnation fleetingly in the top right hand corner of the TV set, but maybe not. Perhaps she had just wanted to for some reason.

Chapter Eleven

A Day in with Mally and Some Robins

Morgan had just about woken up and was in that confused bit where she was wondering about whether what was going through her mind right now was a remnant of a dream or something she ought to be storing in her memory for the future.

There were walls absolutely covered in sheets of newspaper and an extremely bored looking woman standing by a till in what looked like a betting shop containing no customers.

In her earlier dream Morgan remembered that within the steady throng of customers two very different people were using the shop to place their bets at different times and she could pick up on the faint hope and anger of the one extremely fat man as opposed to the quiet desperation of a very smartly dressed be suited man.

Whether this was in fact a dream or a scene from the past or the future was unknown to Morgan right now.

She remembered the fat angry man from the image in her mirror the previous evening and wondered why he was in her thoughts again, but as she was trying to dismiss him from her thoughts, as she still had no empathy for him, she saw a younger version of him holding hands with a good looking young man as they gazed across at Glastonbury Tor together. They looked to be very much in love.

The image then went back to the angrier older and fatter version of the man walking towards the door of the betting shop after counting what she supposed were his winnings.

She was now standing in the street facing the shop with a sprig of lavender in her hand.

The sign outside the shop read 'GH Ruff Turf Accountant', and as she looked up at it until the door opened and she then watched as the fat man emerged in the doorway and proceeded to turn left and walk up the street away from her and the shop with what looked like some considerable difficulty.

As she saw her reflection in the shop window she also saw the beautiful Samoyed Snowbell sitting by her side with two miserable little girls standing between them both. She looked to her right and neither the children nor the dog were beside her, but as she looked back into the reflection in the shop window the image had changed to the two children playing with the smartly suited man who she had seen in the betting shop earlier and who was emitting so much quiet desperation. She then realized he must be the children's father and she guessed that she needed to help him out of whatever problem there was to then help the family that lived at 13 Lavender Crescent.

Just then Mally nuzzled up to Morgan and though there was a brief moment when while she was looking at the smartly suited man there was a loud purring in her right ear and so she conceded she must now be awake, and as she put her right arm out from underneath the duvet to stoke him she decided she had better get up and give the boy his breakfast.

As she was opening the pouch of cat food she looked at her hands and just fleetingly she had the most glamourous long red lacquered fingernails bejewelled with what looked like diamonds.

Morgan pondered whose hands she was seeing while also wondering if she should take herself for a manicure if that could be the stunning end result.

A loud meow indicated that Mally was far more interested in receiving the contents of the pouch that she was still opening and that she was clearly not moving quickly enough for his liking.

Having fed her pal, she wandered over to the telly and switched it on which seemed to disturb a few robins in the foreground of the screen as they flapped their wings.

She then realised the cause of their agitation was behind them. It was a new commercial for Snow Gone Stain Remover that was causing the robins to huddle together for safety now in the bottom left corner of the screen.

It wasn't that the woman in the floaty white dress dancing in a field of white flowers was meant to be remotely scary, it was supposed to be a gentle way of flogging laundry products after all, it was that between twirls and even with her beautiful smile displaying her lovely even white teeth when you looked into her eyes it was as though her soul had gone and not just any stains on her frock.

Morgan had sensed the woman was not right before but now she was even scaring the robins who must know she couldn't possibly hurt them.

She looked into her eyes as she twirled yet again and a deep seated vengeance stared back out at her from the screen. This woman could do something terrible but she had no idea what or even the root cause of the amassed hatred the woman emitted.

As she was having a lazy day at home with Mally she wondered if she might find out who the actress was to see if it would lead her to any clues as to what this was about and why it felt a lot like she would be implicated in whatever was going to happen next.

It transpired she didn't need to look far as at the end of the new advert the line on the screen read 'Elouise always looks her best with Snow Gone'. Not exactly catchy but for some reason Morgan knew they were using the woman's real name.

She could even sense Elouise's disappointment that her name was being used in this way and felt her disappointment at having to sell stain remover, after all if nothing else she was gorgeous.

Mally had walked into the room and hissed at the woman on the telly as he walked past it which further confirmed something was very definitely out of kilter.

Death of a Salesman had pride of place on her coffee table and as the normal dull stream of adverts for beer and cereals was not causing any consternation whatsoever in her home, Morgan decided she would have a cheese and pickle sandwich and make a start on the book so she would know what she was talking about when she reviewed the play for the Chronicle. She was determined to do the best job she could to impress Juliet at the paper as well as James Gazi and not least herself.

She was reading it silently in an American accent and was surprised that she picked up on many of the political themes running throughout the book so quickly.

It wasn't a simple story about greed, it was about demographics, and what constitutes power and achievement as well as how to raise a family to aspiration from hard work. She was enjoying reading the play while making notes immensely.

As she looked casually at her note pad after reading a quarter of the play, she saw the notes she had made about greed, family honour, and loyalty, but she had also subconsciously added a couple of entries which had nothing to do with the book which she had become engrossed in.

'Elouise Fernandez' was written in her hand writing and she knew exactly who that was now but she didn't know the surname until she saw it written down in her own handwriting underneath the word greed and above the word loyalty.

'Maxine's nails' was again written in her own handwriting when she had no memory of writing it, but at least now she knew who the owner of the stunning nails was even if she didn't know anybody called Maxine.

The line was inserted under 'Biff plans to make a business proposition the next day'.

Morgan looked across at the telly which she had been ignoring and watched as a posy of lavender slowly and gracefully made its way from one side of the screen to the other and she guessed this was about Lavender Crescent again.

Right how she was quite happy to read her book, she didn't want all the cryptic signs, just to enjoy reading the book with her Mally for company would do her just fine.

She learned Willy Loman the salesman is 63 years old and very unstable, tending to imagine events from the past as if they are real.

Morgan pondered if that would be better or worse than being interrupted by events in the present and future.

As she continued to read that Willy criticizes Charley and Bernard throughout the play, but it is not because Willy hates them, he finds himself to be jealous of the success gained in their lives and having achieved it without being under Willy's standards, and then a quick glimpse of Elouise Fernandez flashed through her mind involuntarily as she read about the jealousy contained within the play.

Morgan was reading the bit where Willy goes to ask his boss, Howard, for a job in town while Biff goes to make a business proposition, but both fail. Willy gets angry and ends up getting fired when the boss tells him he needs a rest and can no longer represent the company.

At that point the smartly suited man from Lavender Crescent entered her mind's eye again. That was it then, the situation he had put himself in was something to do with employment then presumably, or was she supposed to make him a business proposition? She could overthink the situation for ages but still no answer seemed to be forthcoming, but it was clear to her that the reason she was thinking of him now was precisely down to what she had just read, illogical though that may be.

She continued to read that Biff conveys plainly to his father Willy that he is not meant for anything great, insisting that both of them are simply ordinary men meant to lead ordinary lives.

At that point she put the book back on to the coffee table and closed her eyes for a moment only to see the smartly suited man and the odious fat man she really didn't want to do anything at all for standing outside GH Ruff Turf Accountant with big smiles on their faces.

Well she had not only learnt a fair amount about Death of a Salesman but she had also learnt the reason for, or the solution to, the two mens' current problems was linked to employment or business and most probably concerned a bookies somewhere in London. Great.

It was not going to happening any time soon though so she was going to enjoy the rest of her day off with Mally.

She pulled a book on Churchill out from her bookcase and decided to give it a proper reading next in light of her newly reawakened interest in politics and political figures.

Churchill had famously said, 'History will be kind to me for I intend to write it'. So reading his version of history seemed like an interesting place to start.

While she was thumbing the book another of Churchill's quotes came into her mind:

'Some people regard private enterprise as a predatory tiger to be shot. Others look on it as a cow they can milk. Not enough people see it as a healthy horse, pulling a sturdy wagon'.

Again she saw the signage for GH Ruff Turf Accountant with the two men standing happily outside, but as she looked more closely at the scene a message had been painted on to the shop window in front of a poster of a horse jumping over a fence which had been beautifully caught by the photographer mid-jump. 'Now under new management' the sign simply read.

Morgan shook her head in a concerted effort to get all of these random people that she did not know out of it. This was her day off with Mally after all. She may or may not think over what these people wanted from her at a later date but right now she was going to read a bit on Winston Churchill, maybe read a bit more of Salesman and then she and Mally would put their feet and paws up on the settee and watch a nice upbeat film. Hairspray she thought, scanning her DVD collection. She hadn't had a blast of 'You can't stop the beat' in ages.

After making her and Mally a snack she settled down with some popcorn for them both to share to watch John Travolta in the film which follows the 'pleasantly plump' teenager Tracy Turnblad as she pursues stardom as a dancer on a local TV show and rallies against racial segregation in the early sixties. It was great fun with loads of boppy songs including 'I can hear the bells' and 'Good morning Baltimore'.

They were at the bit where there was a protest, which Tracy's mum Edna has joined at this point, and it is halted by a police roadblock. In an attempt to get an officer's attention, Tracy hits him in the head with a protest sign and the protesters engage in a brawl. While Tracy escapes and hides in a fallout shelter another girl's mother catches Tracy and calls the police before tying her friend Penny to her bed for disobeying her.

It was great fun and Morgan was laughing along and dancing horizontally trough the songs much to Mally's consternation.

Finally the end credits rolled to another chorus of 'You can't stop the beat' which Morgan felt obliged to get up and dance along to, and then she decided it was undoubtedly time for a nice large whisky and milk.

She switched the telly off and as the picture faded it was replaced with a lovely image of Snowbell. Oh okay, she thought, in her now upbeat state of mind, I can't be bothered with the people in all of this but that dog is far too beautiful to ignore.

She sank another even larger measure of whisky with milk while looking out at the beautiful starry sky and thanked the world at large for all the luck in her life especially for giving her such a wonderful friend as Mally.

They went to bed together and Morgan fell asleep to his familiar loud purring as he snuggled up to her.

Sometime must have elapsed before she found herself half-awake in an unfamiliar bed, and when she looked around she found she was in a bed within a bedroom she had never even seen before. She had not woken up and looked down on herself sleeping, nor could she remember having floated here so she surmised that she must be dreaming in her alcohol enhanced sleep.

She rose slightly in the bed and as she looked down at her hands the beautifully painted and bejewelled red fingernails were back. Then, looking to her left, she saw a man she did not at first recognize, but after studying his face for a while she realised it was the man in the smart suit that she had seen earlier outside the bookies, except he was now in flannelette pyjamas.

A faint noise to her right aroused her curiosity and as she looked down by the side of the bed where the noise had emitted from she saw that it was coming from Snowbell who was repositioning himself for more comfort in his sleep. She looked down at her hands again and noticed that she was wearing a golden band on her ring finger. Somehow she had been put into Maxine's position, quite literally.

She looked at the top of the bedside cabinet and saw that a small blue glass dish by the side of the bed contained a scribbled note and she squinted to make out its contents. Beside that was a solitary book which she leant out to touch, but as her hand approached it an aura of light emitted from it and a feeling of heat and power coming off it forced her to pull her hand back away from it. She tried to see the title of the book.

Strangely she felt that she was not in any danger. She pulled herself gently out of bed trying not to wake her husband and walked across to sit at the dressing table facing the mirror. She looked at her reflection and Maxine Spencer stared back at her.

As Morgan looked at the good looking woman before her with her lovely hair she gazed straight into the eyes which they temporarily shared and felt the full gamut of her confused emotions as well as her love and loyalty, not least towards the now asleep husband who was snoring faintly now behind her.

This woman loved her husband and kids and it shone out from her even if she doubted it herself, but she also knew that there was something hugely different about her husband of late. He had not said anything and that made it even worse so she was pondering all sorts of worst case scenarios.

She turned to the slumbering man in the bed and with Maxine's looks and Morgan's voice quietly exclaimed, "You've been an absolute fool at the bank haven't you?" but Roy Spencer slept on unawares.

As Morgan looked back into the mirror she saw her own reflection now and looking back at the bed Maxine was sleeping fitfully alongside her husband while Snowbell snored slightly from beside the bed.

She again looked into the mirror glad to be herself again but rather disappointed at losing Maxine's good looks in the process.

In the background of her reflexion in the mirror her mum's friend Fiona who was looking glamorous in an emerald green crushed velvet dress stood smiling and holding a book in her right hand. Morgan looked back at the bedside table fleetingly and noticed the book which had lain there was now gone but was the same book which Fiona was now holding. This time Morgan saw the cover clearly. The book was titled Seven minutes to win the race, and there was a picture of a beautiful silver horse on the cover.

Fiona smiled and looked directly out at Morgan saying, "Back to bed now Morgan dear, all will become clear another day."

Morgan was awoken again by a loud purring sound and she opened one eye to see Mally gazing lovingly at her and felt the comfort and safety of her own bed. She hugged her pal and fell soundly back to sleep ignoring the bizarre goings which had preceded this moment.

Chapter Twelve

Pickpockets at Work

Stratford was a beautiful place to live and Morgan wouldn't want to live anywhere else in the world and loved the surroundings in which she lived, but being beautiful and cultural it attracted huge volumes of tourists in the spring and summer and with crowds there was always a hiding place for thieves.

Morgan was gazing out of the window of the Stratford Chronicle having already made three good sales to the town's restaurants this morning for advertising space.

There were two casually dressed lads and one fresh faced pretty girl with blonde plaits and a flowery mini skirt walking past the window as she looked on.

Across the road was the Town Hall and she watched as the three friends disappeared within the crowd outside it momentarily. She then watched as the girl lit a cigarette and seemed to be working out her next move at a slight distance from her friends.

Although nothing untoward had happened yet she knew it would in the near future. Without speaking to anyone in the office she checked her Mally was safe by looking in the mirror and seeing that he was happily gazing out of the living room window at home bathed in a patch of sunshine. She made her way to join the throng of people and made herself invisible within them. Instinctively she knew this little group were up to no good and she got the impression they were small time thieves out for what they could get easily from the unsuspecting tourists that were milling around.

As she looked at the girl with the plaits she could see the slight fear in her bright blue eyes and knew that she was just trying to impress one or both of the lads. They in turn could clearly see this and were using her to do their bidding. She was certainly the weak link in this dubious team and Morgan knew she had to concentrate her energies on her.

She was standing behind the girl now who was unaware of her presence. The two lads were somewhere amongst the crowd but invisible to her right now.

She gently put her hand on the girl's shoulder and felt her shaking slightly and she willed her not to object to her hand on her shoulder. She also felt the love emitting from this girl for one of the lads she was with. 'Andy', was all this girl could think about right now and it was for this reason alone that Miranda, who whilst touching her gently Morgan had deduced this love struck girl was, and had reduced her hobbies and standards to small time theft for the sake of a boy.

As she continued to place her hand on her shoulder Morgan willed Miranda to come to her senses. This girl was bright and the apple of her mother's eye with strong morals and many ambitions which she stood every chance of achieving.

She sensed Miranda feeling her mother's contempt and upset at what she was doing and as the girl had now felt the gentle hand on her shoulder she turned around and exclaimed almost pleadingly, "Mum." As she looked straight into Morgan's eyes now she didn't feel embarrassed, as it was as though she could see only her mum Julie's big brown eyes staring out at her from Morgan's eyes, and willing her to stop what she was about to do; and all she could do was stand looking into her mother's eyes and apologising over and over for being so stupid.

Morgan felt slightly odd when the girl hugged her warmly but she knew that it was her mum she was really hugging and so gave Miranda a cuddle in return.

One of the lads had just relieved an unsuspecting tourist of the wallet which was in the back pocket of his jeans. Morgan willed the man to turn around which he did only to see a young man holding his wallet stunned that the guy had noticed. He snatched the wallet back and grabbed the lad by the scruff of the neck and frogmarched him to the other side of the street where two uniformed constables were laughing whilst having a conversation. He then threw the lad at them none too gentle and pointed out to them that the little thug had just tried to rob him. One constable caught hold of the lad and the other asked the tourist some details of what had happened and his telephone number and address.

The police then let the disgruntled tourist go on his pre-booked sightseeing tour bus trip and held on to the now contrite young man who would now be helping them with their enquiries.

Andy was watching from within the crowd as his clingy but malleable would-be-girlfriend was hugging a woman he had never met and his best mate Terry had just been dragged off by the coppers. Today wasn't going to plan for him at all.

He couldn't be bothered pursuing a minor crime spree on his own so wandered away from the thickening crowd and into a café across the road called 'Presto' where he ordered a frothy strawberry milkshake and sat outside waiting for Miranda to see him there and come over to join him.

She did actually look rather fit today in her short skirt with her great long legs he had to admit.

He had plenty of cash on him anyway and he only went along with Terry for the thrill of the chase and to manipulate Miranda to do his bidding, but really he came from a clean living family of solicitors and barristers and just wanted to do something fun that would preferably upset his straight-laced successful father into the bargain if he ever got caught.

Morgan was chatting to Miranda for quite some time on the other side of the road and he watched as they made each other laugh while chatting easily now. Thinking about it he had never made her laugh quite like that and bizarrely that made him suddenly feel quite jealous.

He caught her eye and beckoned her over to the café, but whereas up until recently she would have been there in an instant, this time she looked at him dismissively and carried on with her conversation.

Morgan certainly didn't claim to be able to cure love related issues, but just chatting to the lovely girl before her she knew now how clever and funny she was and also what a total prat she now felt for being roped in to

Andy's hair brain scheme which was utterly beneath her. It was as though the scales had suddenly lifted from her eyes and Andy was no longer a love interest, but instead he was a puffed up moron who could have got them all arrested.

Morgan and Miranda were now chatting like firm friends and when Morgan said she worked for the Stratford Chronicle Miranda was hugely impressed and told her that she wanted to become a journalist one day, writing fashion articles preferably.

Two pigeons were now standing by their feet overseeing proceedings and as Morgan was in no great hurry to sit back opposite Rose's miserable face she suggested she stood them both a coffee and nodded across to the forlorn looking Andy who was staring miserably at his milkshake. "I think he might appreciate you a bit more from now on," said Morgan, and Miranda giggled as they crossed the road to join Andy outside the café still attended by the two pigeons.

Morgan ordered the coffees while Miranda sat down next to Andy who said he was sorry while looking at his trainers. He didn't offer any further words but smiled at her very fondly.

Walking over to the pair with the coffees Morgan was chuffed when Miranda introduced her to Andy as her new friend.

"He's actually very clever," said Miranda by way of apologising for Andy's behaviour. "All of his family are in the law business."

Andy looked slightly embarrassed, but as Morgan shook his hand she knew that one day he too aspired to be a barrister or solicitor so looking straight into his eyes she said, "And you absolutely will be taking the silk one day too I'm sure."

Andy seemed relieved by what was more of a statement of fact than small talk and he felt he was being told the path of his life by a trustworthy source.

The three chatted for a while with the pigeons happily weaving between their feet and fluttering about while picking up crumbs left by earlier customers.

They had just finished their drinks when an extremely contrite looking Terry sat down at the table and muttered that he had just accepted a caution from the police.

"I think it's safe to say we've all now moved on from this now," said Miranda looking at Morgan. "I'll get us another round in, what are you having Terry?"

Morgan put her hand across to Terry and he shook it. As they touched for some reason she knew that Terry would go on to be a talented mechanic. This little group weren't bad people at all, in fact they were making Morgan feel very young herself right now by being in their company.

Looking out of the mirror opposite them within the café and gazing lovingly at Miranda, a classy and smartly dressed lady with hair styled like the late Princess Diana, who Morgan presumed to be Julie was smiling broadly across to her daughter and the expression of calmness and relief on her face was evident, as was the love she held for this young woman she had brought up.

A couple of robins were toddling about in the foreground of the mirror until a pair of pigeons landed within the frame and they fluttered out of their way rather grudgingly.

Morgan drank her coffee and thought about going back to work to bring in some money for Mally's preference for fine dining.

Glancing back up to the mirror she could see her dad looking back at her out of it now and she was surprised to notice how frail he was. It was as if there was the young dad that gave her piggy backs and took her swimming and now the frail little old man, but she couldn't recall the transition between the two of them. It was the bright blue eyes that showed the subtle difference, once twinkling with energy and humour and now, though still showing intelligence the energy and effort for life, appeared to be waning and the twinkle diminishing.

There was distinct contrast as Morgan looked back around the table to these three young chums that had seemed to readily adopt her as a friend. She felt gratitude for both her father's love and her new chum's faith and acceptance in her and decided they needed cakes at a time like this, the more cream and jam with chocolate in them the better. She would look out for these kids as best she could from now on and would enjoy watching their progress from a distance, although she would try to get Miranda some work experience at the chronicle if she could.

Looking back in the mirror with some trepidation she again saw her dad, but this time he was leaning it looked somewhat painfully on a blue wheelie bin which his cat Tabby was sitting on and looking up at him lovingly.

She looked into his eyes and silently willed him to understand just how much she loved him.

The young group around her were chatting cheerily amongst themselves freely and happily now and it was as though a barrier to their friendship had been lifted now that they had mutually acknowledged that they did not need to resort to petty crime and bravado to impress each other, it was much easier for them to just be proper mates.

They were talking about the latest film release due to be showing at the cinema from Friday and they were deciding where and when to meet up before watching Spy, which looked like begin a really funny film as it starred the talented and comedic Melissa McCarthy in the lead playing a spoof version of a James Bond type CIA Agent. Morgan had read a review in the Sunday newspaper and it did look like great fun to her.

She shared what she had read with her new friends and casually mentioned though rather too proudly that she was currently reviewing Arts and Entertainment for the Stratford Chronicle.

It got one of those impressed looks from Miranda which was exactly what she was aiming for although she didn't understand quite why she needed to impress this girl so much.

"Jason Statham is apparently really funny in it and it's got Jude Law for eye candy," mused Morgan.

"Bit old for me," laughed Miranda in good nature, but making Morgan feel her age again.

"What am I going to tell my folks about this caution?" asked Terry who was obviously still reeling from the experience.

Miranda looked across at him and said, "Why tell them anything? Just make them proud of you instead."

They were wise words for one so young.

"I think I will start work on that old Vespa that I bought as a project and never did anything about. Yeah, I'll do a fantastic job of doing it up…"

Terry's father John was a mechanic who had been a marshal on RAC rallies in the past as well as working with the Williams Formula 1 Team. He had only given up the later due to developing an alcohol addiction which had changed their happy family unit from one all about engines to something no longer recognisable as a functional family and involving much shouting, slurping, silly accusations, and a great many tears from his mother Mandy.

Lately though John was getting some help and admitting he had a problem and he spent a great deal more time sober, and when he and Terry had their little one to one conversations about cars and racing Terry was always in awe and so proud of his dad and his abilities with motors.

Now it was his turn. He would totally strip the Vespa down, rebuild the engine, and make the bodywork beautiful. That would make his old dad proud and it would help on his CV when he applied for a job as a mechanic in the future. Yes, all was well, even exciting. "In fact, no time like the present," and Terry bounced up and shook everyone's hands while bidding them farewell and removing sugar from the corner of his mouth. As he shook Morgan's hand he gave her a cheeky wink and she could feel while holding his hand briefly what a gentle lad he was.

That left Morgan with the newly contrite Andy, who was gazing across at Miranda adoringly while talking about the latest song he had downloaded to his iPad.

As she was now surplus to requirements she too made her exit back across the road to the chronicle after wishing the pair a good day and genuinely telling them how pleased she was to meet them.

She had just got back into the office when a surly looking Rose asked if she was going to do any work that day. Not that it was any of her business and she had made more sales than her no doubt before she had even gone out.

Ignoring the barb, she walked over to the mirror seemingly to put her hair straight but really checking her Mally was still alright. He was sitting on the sunny spot by the window watching two pigeons extremely intently which were getting a bit too close for his comfort on the other side of it. She smiled at the image of her pal.

Walking back to her desk she watched as Miranda and Andy wandered down the opposite side of the road linked together by the speakers of the iPad. They stopped momentarily when Andy made Miranda roar with laughter and ambled along together hand in hand pursued at a short distance by the two pigeons that had followed them from the café. They had appeared to have adopted this young couple as their charges.

Rose got up and silently and begrudgingly put a note on to Morgan's desk. It read:

'Presto café opposite us wish to advertise for the next three weeks. Please ask the nice red haired woman who was here earlier to pop in again and agree the terms and pricing with Sue, the manager.'

Morgan smiled at the precious little effort her job generally involved. She would take herself over there for another coffee the next time she got a bit thirsty and fancied a stroll. Then she would pop up the road and see if the new 'Hawaii' boutique would like to advertise with her. She had forgotten all about them until an image of herself in a floaty blue floral blouse with a lovely pattern made up of bluebells with one of their 'Hawaii' tags with a pink palm tree on it had entered her head. She looked rather lovely in the blouse of her vision and she wondered if she could negotiate a discount with them at the same time as getting some more advertising space sold. She might even bring back some cakes to put a smile onto Rose's miserable face while she was on her feet.

Chapter Thirteen

The Audition Result

Elouise Fernandez had been tossing and turning all night interspersed with dreams about stardom and failure. Since the last dream had involved her becoming a huge success she looked across at her alarm clock which displayed the time as 6.00am and decided that while in a content but nervous state of mind she might as well give up on the concept of more sleep and start preparing for the job interview which was in her mind the make or break opportunity which would define the rest of her life.

She poured herself some extremely strong black coffee and pondered what outfit would be most suitable for this occasion. She decided on a figure hugging black satin dress teamed with a red feather boa and red patent leather stilettos to enhance her legs and ensure that her image would be memorable.

She sat in front of the dressing table mirror and saw herself as a blank canvas which would need a lot of effort with her make-up to make her look utterly stunning.

On the dressing table lay the envelope containing the invite to her audition for the lead role in Evita that contained the letter which elated her every time she had looked at it, and that had been around three times a day since it had first landed through her letterbox.

The first time she had read it she had squealed with the excitement and every time she had looked at it since her heart had leapt and she felt butterflies as well as pride and hope.

She simply had to get this role. It was all she had ever wanted and this was finally the opportunity she had dreamed of. All she had to do was look wonderful and act and sing even more wonderfully throughout the audition. She must not blow this. Her hands and body were starting to shake with a mixture of passion and determination. It was inconceivable to her that she may not get the job: That simply didn't figure.

Her immaculately applied make-up was more dramatic than usual and she had taken her time so that it enhanced her looks to perfection.

She put her hair up in a stylish chignon making her look classy and after applying her trademark pillar box red lipstick she completed the effect with a large squirt of 'Siren' perfume which was her mother's favourite going out scent and which she wore when she needed to feel her mum's presence around her. Today she needed to impress her mum so much.

The interview venue was less than a mile away and Elouise thought a bit of fresh air before her appointment would do her good and clear her head of any negativity.

The audition was being held at the tiny Minniack Theatre and as she approached the shabby emerald green stage door with its chipped paint she was spurred on by a wolf whistle which was aimed her way from the trio of builders working on the ornate shop front of a jewellery shop across the road from the theatre.

She smiled coyly back at them as she opened the door and was then greeted by a pretty blonde girl who was holding a clipboard. The girl walked over to Elouise from behind the reception desk and asked if she was her for an audition. When she confirmed she was and also confirmed her name which the girl noted on her list Elouise craned her neck in an attempt to see how many other candidates she was up against. But the girl only ticked her name off in a matter of seconds before holding the clipboard tightly to her chest while giving her the smiley instruction to please follow her. She still didn't know what the opposition looked like or how numerous they were.

Sarah, as she fleetingly announced herself with a backward glance which didn't make eye contact, took Elouise onto the stage and announced her presence to the three nonplussed people sitting behind bizarrely archaic small desks which had newly engraved name plaques sitting on each.

They were sitting huddled in the corner of the small stage deliberately taking up as little room as possible so as to give their auditonees as much room as possible to present their talents, or not as the case may be.

The poor dull grey haired and dull grey looking pianist looked bored rigid and that was before anybody had even spoken.

Sarah sashayed off the stage wishing Elouise a very smiley good luck while still holding the clipboard tight to her chest and the three interviewers spoke and announced themselves from behind the desks which would not have looked out of place in the classroom of a junior school.

Nearest to Elouise sat Nick Cameron who announced that he was the Casting Director for this production of Evita. As he smiled willingly Elouise wondered if this was the same Nick Cameron who had flatly turned her down to represent her as her agent and she also wondered if this was the case if her remembered her name at all.

Nick introduced Roger Floyd the Production Director who was sitting next to him and who raised his eyes fleetingly to meet hers and then continued to read something on a piece of paper which was on the desk in front of him.

At the end of the row sat Abbey Jukes the Company Manager who got up and shook hands across the desk with Elouise. She was extremely young thought Elouise but at least seemed friendly.

Walking from the wings at the right of the stage and approaching Elouise was a man walking with an exaggerated saunter who looked in bad need of a shave.

"And this is our leading man," said Abbey with clear pride. "Max Perini has already been cast in the role of Che Guevara and wanted to sit in on the auditions to find his leading lady. You don't mind do you?"

Elouise would have been pretty stupid to say yes, so instead she put on her most enigmatic smile and come-hither eyes and shook his hand for just a little too long.

Abbey handed Elouise a copy of the poem 'If' by Rudyard Kipling and as the three interviewers sat behind their desks with Max drooped over the back of Abbey's chair Nick Cameron asked her to stand in the middle of stage and read the poem out in full to the non-existent audience.

Elouise had her songs and lyrics from Evita rehearsed over and over to perfection but this exercise had just been bounced on her and seemed rather pointless, much like when she had once applied to be a Saturday shop assistant when she first left school and was asked to bring a SWOT Analysis of the pokey boutique with her when she attended the interview. She had written many lines about up-selling and understanding the target market and subsequently failed to get the job, which by then she didn't want as it was a ridiculous process involving talking in pointless big words for no real reason.

As Elouise stood with the poem before her it was as though Nick Cameron had read her mind. "This is to test your projection and annunciation," he declared.

Looking out into the darkness Elouise began:

"If you can keep your head when all about you
Are losing theirs and blaming it on you,
If you can trust yourself when all men doubt you,
But make allowance for their doubting too;
If you can wait and not be tired by waiting,
Or being lied about, don't deal in lies,
Or being hated, don't give way to hating,
And yet don't look too good, nor talk too wise:

"If you can dream - and not make dreams your master;
If you can think - and not make thoughts your aim;
If you can meet with Triumph and Disaster
And treat those two impostors just the same;
If you can bear to hear the truth you've spoken
Twisted by knaves to make a trap for fools,
Or watch the things you gave your life to, broken,
And stoop and build 'em up with worn-out tools"

"She was conscious of forming every word perfectly and expounding on every meaning and thought her projection and delivery was at just the right volume for all of the non-existent audience to hear. She put added passion into the final verse just to drive the message home.

"If you can talk with crowds and keep your virtue,
Or walk with Kings - nor lose the common touch,
if neither foes nor loving friends can hurt you,
If all men count with you, but none too much;
If you can fill the unforgiving minute
With sixty seconds' worth of distance run,
Yours is the Earth and everything that's in it,
And - which is more - you'll be a Man, my son!"

When nobody said anything she walked back to the panel to just the sound of her stilettos clicking on the stage and handed Abbey back the poem and then Max and Abbey give her a short token round of applause. Elouise noted that Max was still slouching and couldn't help thinking that the poem could certainly not have been written about him. He was sloppy and unkempt but right now he would need to think that Elouise found him charming and captivating.

The audition then continued exactly as Elouise had wanted it to go from the outset.

This was what she excelled at.

She informed the pianist that she would be singing 'What's new Buenos Aires?' and 'Don't cry for me Argentina', from the show and walked back to the centre of the stage to sing them, but this time she was facing the panel and she meant every word she sang: The power, the passion and the ambition were all hers from within.

She envisaged the young Eva Peron about to embark on her great adventure as she sang:

"I get out here, Buenos Aires
Stand back, you oughta know whatcha gonna get in me
Just a little touch of star quality
Fill me up with your heat, with your noise
With your dirt, overdo me
Let me dance to your beat, make it loud
Let it hurt, run it through me.
Don't hold back, you are certain to impress
Tell the driver this is where I'm staying."

And then the wonderful theme tune music of her life started and she launched straight into a powerful rendition of 'Don't cry for me Argentina', sincerely meaning the opening line:

"I had to let it happen, I had to change, couldn't spend all my life down at heel looking out of the window and staying out of the sun."

She sang the entire song beautifully and with strength and power of delivery and completed the song with a heartfelt, "All you have to do is look at me to know that every word it is true."

And every word of those two songs had never been so important or meaningful to Elouise as it was right now. She had sung note perfect and could do no more. She looked hopefully back at the panel where Abbey and Max smiled gently back at her and they had all seemed attentive as she had sung.

She wished they would react like Pauline always did when she had been with The Beaudesert Players. She would have been on her feet by now grinning and clapping and praising Elouise for being so brilliant. Elouise so missed that reaction especially at an odd and awkward moment of silence such as now.

Nick stood up and shook hands with Elouise while thanking her for her time and saying she would receive a formal written response after they had seen all of the candidates. Roger then also shook her hand followed by Abbey who at least gave her a proper smile. Max lolloped around the desks until he was in front of her giving her a lopsided smile followed by a kiss on the cheek which she hoped she looked appreciative of, and then there was just the sound of her heels clip-clopping across the stage, and then she was alone as she walked back past the now unmanned reception desk and out into the bright sunshine through the shabby green stage door. There was nothing more she could do now but wait. She had given it her all and would now find a decent hostelry where she would consume a few large whiskies to restore her jagged nerves before going home and waiting for a formal response to fall through her letterbox.

Morgan Martin was utterly unaware of what was happening in Elouise's life and even less concerned as she awoke to bright sunlight streaming in through the bedroom window and consuming Mally in its glow, who was sitting contently on the duvet and purring loudly.

Morgan had had a lovely night's sleep and had not floated anywhere, in fact the only dream she could recollect was about a lovely meal she had at the Mayflower Chinese restaurant a couple of years ago which was memorable because it was one of the rare times she and her friend Jennifer got together.

She stretched, got up, and dressed in a shocking pink mohair jumper and her comfiest jeans and trundled downstairs to put the kettle on and to give Mally his breakfast.

The milk float was just driving past her front window as she was making her cup of coffee which was timely, so she went to collect the two bottles of milk which would have just been left for her outside of the front door.

As she opened the door bright sunlight again flooded into her house and a blackbird with what looked like a small white patch on its head stood a few feet away observing her quizzically.

She said good morning to the bird and picked both bottles of milk up. One seemed to vibrate its way away from her hand and though the bottle had not broken the foil cap had come off and the milk was slowly spilling its contents over the doormat.

She had had a good grip on the bottle. It was as though some force had taken it back out of her hand and for a moment Morgan was very cautious that something was about to happen.

This was not without foundation. On the morning of the 9/11 terror attacks in America Morgan had begun the day in the same seemingly innocuous way. She had picked up the milk and one bottle had appeared to pull itself away from her through vibration. She had watched the contents spilling away that time but didn't know it meant anything other than more black coffee than usual.

On that day she had then switched the television on to see the iconic images of two planes flying into the

World Trade Center which would subsequently fall down taking so many innocent lives with it.

It was therefore with some trepidation that she switched the telly on as she feared something terrible may have happened in the World.

It seemed to be a commercial break but the image of Elouise Fernandez in the Stain Gone advert was not moving. Morgan switched the set top box on and off and still the image had not changed.

The black bird with its white patch was now standing in front of the image of Elouise but behind the screen and acting as though it had got trapped and was scared. There was nothing that Morgan could do but look on.

The odd scene was interrupted momentarily when the postman stuck something through the letterbox and Morgan walked into the hall to find a white DL envelope addressed to her which she pondered without opening for a moment. Again it felt as if there was an energy coming off it and not necessarily in a good way.

The phone in the hall rang then and just briefly as Morgan lifted the receiver she heard her mother's voice clearly warning her to be careful and especially in London and then the voice was replaced by some sales girl asking her if she could replace one, two or three windows which ones would they be?

Morgan politely said she was not interested but was quietly annoyed the girl's voice had replaced her mothers, but it was nice to know she was still there for her somewhere.

She looked out of the front window and saw the black bird with its white patch standing on the front lawn looking in at her and occasionally daring to glance in the area of the telly. Morgan neither knew how it had got in or got back out again but it seemed there was something far more sinister happening as the image of Elouise was growing in size behind the screen until just her face filled the entire screen with her huge eyes now black as the pupils had dilated so much. Her red lipstick looked immaculate but those eyes looked possessed. It was as if she were fit to kill. Mally cowered in a corner of the room and Morgan didn't know what to do. She really did not want this woman in her house.

She remembered the letter she had left by the phone and went to fetch it by means of a distraction. As she picked it up she felt a surge of anger, betrayal and disappointment like she had never felt and as she looked back at the telly she saw that Elouise although deranged through anger now had a lone tear falling down her cheek.

Opening the envelope, she saw that she had won a twenty-pound gift voucher for entering a crossword competition which made for a pleasant interlude from whatever was happening.

The image of Elouise was now fading into the breakfast TV and soon it was gone much to the relief of both Morgan and Mally, who finally dared to come out of his corner. The black bird was still watching in but gave a little song and appeared much more contented.

At home in London Elouise Fernandez had just received a letter from the postman and had put the DL envelope to one side until she had made a strong coffee so that there could be a proper ceremony of the opening of the envelope.

She tentatively and carefully opened the envelope to find a sheet of headed paper titled Cameron Musical Productions. She read every word slowly so as not to miss anything and when she had repeated the process twice she had never felt such a rage and absolute sense of disappointment and futility as she did right now.

Chapter Fourteen

Ted Clarke to Parliament

Ted Clarke had awoken with the flu. As if he didn't feel sorry for himself enough he now had an additional reason to be miserable.

Ted now had the ideal reason to feel more sympathy for himself than anyone else in the world. The only plus points were that the flu was making him less aware of his arthritis and he was unlikely to leave his flat anytime soon so would delay being called an effing elephant followed by smug giggling or whatever the favourite insult of the day would be from the youths that seemed to be permanently lurking in wait to verbally abuse him outside his own home.

He looked up at the ceiling and dozed a little longer until he heard the paper boy sticking his Racing Post Weekender through the letterbox. That was one small reason to get out of bed in due course, the thought of backing some winners. He was quite good at that really.

He hadn't got much food in so thought he might have a cheese and tomato pizza for breakfast-cum-lunch if he could face it. He then lay in bed pondering why they never put enough cheese on them and why it never reached anywhere close to the edges.

Not getting an answer to either of these big questions he decided he probably ought to get up.

Coughing his way across to the hall he picked up the Weekender as well as a Daily Mail which had been wrongly delivered. It had no number written on it or he would have put it through to the correct address. Instead he flicked through it and on page 5 noticed a picture of the non-communicative and horribly smug looking Grant Ruffelle MP with his arm around what he supposed was his wife. It was not a fond embrace though, more of an ear-marking of property and the property didn't look too enamoured with his company for that matter.

His eyes casually moved to the headline above it and all thoughts of how ill he was had suddenly vanished to be replaced by the slow boiling of his blood and increased loathing of this vile toff.

'Ruffelle opposes gay marriage as being abnormal' was the headline, and as Ted read the article beneath the couple pictured it became clear that Grant Ruffelle MP had given an 'exclusive' interview to the Mail detailing his 'preference for marriage between a man and a woman'. As Ted glanced back at the photo it was not remotely clear that he was actually in a happy marriage. The article went on about 'Christian beliefs' and 'Family units which would confuse any children' as well as apparently what was simply an incorrect message for society and an unnatural practice being condoned by too many.

Ted could not believe this man actually thought such vile things, let alone was prepared for his disgusting prejudice to be published for anybody to see.

Richard had died long before gay marriage was on any government's agenda, but in all but paper they were married and were a devoted couple and Ted was quite sure that if marriage had been an option in their day they would have discussed the matter seriously.

Not only was Ruffelle a useless politician who had still not responded to two of Ted's letters, he was also calling the main reason for his existence and the one great thing that had happened in his life unnatural and abnormal. Ted's love for Richard had been neither of these things, it had been sincere and wonderful.

By way of calming himself down he made himself a coffee and sat analysing the horses in his Weekender. He then made a list of prospective winners to back next time his was near the bookies.

He glanced at the non-committal letter from the MP which sat on the coffee table and vowed to let the moron know just how offensive he was whether or not that meant being rehomed to somewhere without stairs. He would go to parliament and confront him if necessary. Not only was he being ignored he was now being insulted by this idiot whose wages he was paying to do nothing for him.

Morgan was looking at Ted Clarke pottering in his flat in the mirror in her hall and while she still didn't warm to him she certainly now appreciated he was actually a caring man underneath all of his bulk, and she had watched as he had read the offending article in the paper and then circled his potential winning horses in the Weekender. She hoped they did win for him, the man could do with a break by the looks of it and she didn't know anything about Mr Ruffelle but he appeared to be a very worthy recipient of Ted's vitriol.

The now familiar image of fat Ted slowly vanished to be replaced by that of a lovely chocolate coloured whippet with big brown eyes which was whimpering slightly as though it was in a bit of pain. This was a far more important issue to Morgan and she willed the dog to tell her what was wrong and where it was, which of course it didn't. It was joined in the mirror by its friend who was a lighter beige coloured whippet with a lovely shinny coat who gave the other dog a friendly slurp on the nose with his tongue.

Morgan had been thinking of Grant Ruffelle when these two dogs had appeared and she wondered momentarily if there was a connection there.

Ted's vendetta with the man had been clearly in her thoughts when this pair had looked out at her balefully and as she continued to watch she saw that one was called Wallaby and the other Koala from the brass bone shaped tags attached to their pink leather collars.

Morgan stood back from the mirror to try and get a more panoramic view of the room which the dogs were in and an idea of where they were.

Whilst she couldn't see the entire room as yet a shrill voice came out from the left hand side of the mirror, "Have you kicked Wally or Coco again you bully?" followed by an uncaring voice coming from the right hand side of the mirror,

"They're only bloody dogs Claudia, the stupid things keep getting under my feet."

Morgan could now see the full, expensively decorated room from the safe vantage point of her mirror and immediately recognised Grant Ruffelle and his wife from the image in Ted's newspaper.

The conversation appeared to have now stopped and the pair were now ignoring each other while sitting on separate plush sofas displaying embroidered Latin quotes written on them in a gold thread on a burgundy background. For all of the beauty of the room the pair did not seem remotely content in each other's company.

"Don't forget we're going out for dinner at that new Bangladeshi restaurant tonight Claudia, make sure you look good won't you."

The attractive but rather cold seeming Claudia sneered back, "I'd hate not to look pristine for you in front of the foreigners you can't stand my love," and another few moments of silent stand-off followed.

Grant Ruffelle got up then and the two dogs huddled together when he did so, as if protecting each other. Morgan wondered just what he had done to make them need to. They were stunning dogs with gorgeous glossy coats which proved they must be cared for if not loved wholeheartedly.

There was a horrible air of uncaring about this whole set up. As Grant and Claudia were still giving each other the silent treatment Morgan scanned the elegant room they were in. The décor was stylish and beautiful but the framed photos contained formal images of the MP in stiffly formal poses shaking hands with what Morgan guessed were important people to him. The only picture of Claudia in the room was a small one on a side table showing their wedding and even that looked too formal to show any sincerity.

Grant broke the silence by saying, "I'll take the dogs for a walk round the market." It was an excuse to get out as Claudia knew this full well as she told him that she was getting her hair done and not to rush back without even looking at him once.

The two dogs looked across at Morgan through the mirror and she winked back at them as they were put on their leads and went out of the room with the MP.

The image then faded from the mirror and Morgan was now looking at her own reflection which showed Mally watching her unblinkingly from the arm of the settee in the living room behind her. She was glad to leave the room and its antagonistic atmosphere behind but was still more than a bit concerned for the safety of those lovely dogs.

Ted Clarke was feeling slightly less like death by now. He had eaten a whole cheese and tomato pizza even though there was not enough cheese on it and what there was made it nowhere near to the edges, he was now back to studying the form for this afternoons racing. He would put a little bet on Mowgli in the 2.30pm at Kempton he thought. The horse was 28 – 1 and stood little chance, but he did so miss Albi's lovely black chow chow who he had fussed over so many times with Richard.

He could even fancy taking himself out for a couple of pints later subject to winning them first of course.

A Jehovah's Witness disturbed his analysing of form then by knocking on the door. Ted looked at the timid woman on the doorstep and smiled at her. "I'm very busy but if you leave me a magazine I'll read it." The woman handed him a Watchtower and said that she hoped that he would enjoy reading it and then she was gone.

Ted put the magazine on his coffee table for perusal later. He would read it, but more out of disbelief at how other people thought than for his own religious instruction.

Ted wrote down his top bets for the day and decided a spot of fresh air and a slow stroll to the bookies would do him a power of good, especially if he had picked all of the winners of course.

He eventually struggled into GH Ruff Turf Accountant and placed his bets with what looked to be a pleasant new girl behind the counter, she even gave him a smile when handing him his betting slips. Service was looking up.

He parked himself on a stool and watched all of the races he had backed on. They were only win singles but some of them were going to go off at quite long prices.

The first race he watched was the one with Mowgli in. He didn't hold out much hope as it was a bet based on sentiment more than anything else, so he was chuffed to bits when the horse pulled three lengths clear going into the final furlong and then extended the lead to win comfortably by five lengths. He even forgot his arthritis and flu as he smiled and waved his arms in the air. Mowgli had romped home at 28 – 1 with £ 2.00 to win on him. The new recruit smiled across at him from behind the counter and he gave her a thumps up sign and a smile in return. The afternoon got even better. He had backed a further four winners at prices ranging from 4 -1 to 16 – 1 and the horse he packed that had fallen over was on his feet and looked fine which was the most important thing. This was possibly Ted's best betting day in years and he was thrilled when Jeanie, as she introduced herself, the new cashier, offered him a coffee at a quiet time and came and had a chat with him between races. She made the place much friendlier. As it had been an enjoyable and profitable afternoon Ted said a friendly cheerio to Jeanie and decided it must be time for a decent pint of beer.

As he approached the bar in the 'Old Nag' the be-suited gentleman he had met previously in the pub tapped him gentle on the shoulder. "What would you like to drink sir?" he politely enquired. "You were right about Stately Pride at Kempton, so I can afford to live for another week. I recommend the Red Goblin ruby bitter."

"Why not?" shrugged Ted and the two men enjoyed a pint of Red Goblin each and a chat about where Stately Pride may run next time out.

They were sitting by the window as Ted needed a sit down and Roy Spencer glanced out of it and declared back to Ted in disbelief, "I'm sure I just saw that man kick one of his dogs."

Ted had missed whatever had happened and said benignly, "I can't stand people being cruel to animals."

The door to the pub opened and Grant Ruffelle walked over to the bar with a slightly aloof and arrogant manner about him, wearing an expensive grey tailored suit and trailing two dogs behind him. He ordered a gin and tonic without making eye contact with the barmaid, threw a pile of coins on the bar so the barmaid had to help herself to the right money, scooped up the remainder of the pile of cash and sat at the nearest table without bothering to look at anybody else.

Roy leaned across to Ted and said in hushed tones "That's the man who kicked his dog."

Looking across the room Ted recognised Grant Ruffelle immediately. The two dogs by his feet were beautiful but cowering. Ted thought about telling the man what a tosser he was but decided he probably already knew he was one.

He remembered the anti-gay comments he had made as well as the bland response to his plight which still sat on his coffee table, but instead he decided he would rather have a pint and a chat with his new friend.

Ted kept half an eye on his nemesis though as he and Roy discussed the merits of all-weather racecourses.

Out of the corner of his eye Ted saw Grant telling one of the dogs to stop bloody getting under his feet and he turned to see the man kick the dog firmly in the belly causing it to yelp loudly from under the table.

That was it. Ted was on his feet and across to the table quicker than he had moved in the last two decades. "You will not treat those dogs like that. Nobody has the right to mistreat an animal like that."

Grant Ruffelle, who was not used to being directly challenged, sat silently staring at the fat man as a small crowd formed and fell silent around them waiting for the next move.

The words were out of Ted's mouth before he had even realised he intended to say them. "It would be unsafe to leave those dogs with you for a minute longer. They are coming home with me for their safety."

Grant really should have put up more of a protest as he knew Claudia preferred the dogs to him, but he would be more than happy to see the back of them if truth be told.

Ted walked right up to Grant and demanded he hand over the leads there and then.

Aware he was surrounded and being watched Grant now thought about how best to quietly get out of this place before anybody recognised him.

Ted continued in as brave a voice as he could muster, "I know who you are and if you don't hand those dogs over to me now I'll go to the press about this."

Grant being the selfish coward he was downed his drink, handed over the dogs on their leads and walked back out of the pub in a slightly less aloof manner without looking back once at the dogs.

When he had gone the group of people who had been watching applauded and when he looked around Roy was also clapping. He went bright red with embarrassment but it did feel good. He looked down to see four beautiful big eyes looking back up at him and he made a point of making a big fuss of both of the dogs.

He got a couple of pints in and he and Roy enjoyed a pint of Red Goblin each and they both had a dog's head resting gently on their feet. The dogs looked contented and Roy and Ted now moved on to discussing the favourite food of Roy's dog Snowbell and the nearest place to buy a couple of dog beds.

It hadn't been a day that Ted had expected to end so well when he woke up feeling ill, but now he had a new friend and two lovely dogs as well as a spot of cash so it was pretty close to a perfect day by now.

Grant Ruffelle was sitting at a lacquered table at the new Bangladeshi restaurant 'Noshi' opposite his attractive but non-conversational wife eating some unidentifiable foreign food and pondering what to tell her had happened to the dogs. He hadn't yet worked out a convincing enough lie but he would think of something credible and probably before their desserts arrived.

Outside the pub Ted bade Roy farewell and walked his new friends which he had already renamed Tom and Jerry in his head back to his flat with something like a spring in his step. He was actually looking forward to going home now he had his lovely new pals. He stopped off at the pet shop and bought the food as recommended by Roy as well as bowls and two very snuggly looking dog beds and knew he would enjoy spending the evening in with Tom and Jerry for company.

A kid called him a giant jelly when Ted was nearly home but he couldn't give a monkeys as he let the dogs into his flat and welcomed them to their new home. He put the beds down in a corner of the living room and the food and new bowls in the kitchen before walking back to the coffee table and screwing the letter from Grant Ruffelle into a ball for the dogs to play with. He smiled as they happily played together and occasionally came back to him for a fuss.

Ted sat down to watch them and gave the Watchtower he had been given earlier a perusal as he had promised he would.

As he read 'I will never leave you and I will never abandon you' it took on a whole new meaning now a soggy nose was sticking out from underneath the bottom of the magazine and he was given a lick to infer his attention was required elsewhere

He continued to read that 'Each day has enough of its own troubles' and up until today he would have concurred, but his flat now felt like the happiest place he could possibly be.

Ted was even less sure about, 'Jehovah will always help us along as we keep seeking to do his will' he would just do his best to do right by Tom and Jerry from now on.

He did chuckle slightly at, 'Let your way of life be free of the love of money while you are content with the present things'. That was exactly how he felt right now, although, to be fair, the nice win on the horses had added to his cracking day.

This flat was no longer a place he wanted to get away from. He tore the Watchtower apart page by page and made a number of screwed up balls for his new pals who were having a field day playing with them.

Grant Ruffelle had unwittingly given him the idyllic home life he had craved for way too long, stairs or no stairs.

Morgan Martin watched the happy tableau unseen from the mirror in her hall with a big smile on her face and wondered why she hadn't thought of this.

Chapter Fifteen

A Flying Visit to Dad

Morgan was just thinking about having a drink and settling down to watch the soaps. She had done a stint at the Chronicle and had shifted a fair bit of advertising space, but in that entire time nobody had mentioned her preferred vocation as an Arts Correspondent even though Juliet Moore had walked past her twice that day and had just said 'Hi' on both occasions. On her way out she had heard mutterings about Sammy being able to return to work soon and then felt a tad guilty as she wished her to have another accident of some sort that rendered her unable to write yet again.

It was nice just to have a sit down with Mally and forget about the place. She stroked his head and listened to his contented purring and all was once again well in the world, but not for long.

Her mother's voice was suddenly extremely clear in her head as she said worriedly, "You need to look after your dad, Morgan. Somethings now right. There's nothing I can do so you're going to have to, okay?"

And then the purring was back, but even though the voice had only come from inside her own head Morgan had absolutely no doubt that it was very real indeed.

Morgan went straight to the phone in the hall to ring her dad and the ringing went on for ages until she conceded nobody was going to answer it at the other end.

She looked up to see a very concerned looking Tabby staring back at her from the mirror and quietly asked, "Where is he Tabby, and what has happened?"

Tabby nuzzled the frame of the mirror and then wandered backwards and forwards across the length of it while throwing Morgan the odd concerned look and occasional perturbed sounding meow. Morgan looked on for a while helpless as to what else to do. She then poured herself a glass of wine and hoped that it would help her to formulate a plan. "What am I going to do about my dad, your grandad, pal?" She asked Mally, who looked back at her sympathetically but did not give an answer.

She gingerly went back to the mirror while still holding the glass of cheap claret left over from Christmas because it was so horrible and was taking rather large sips as she was scared, but as she was now standing further away from it so as to get a better view of what was in the distance she saw that in the background from Tabby. There was a blue wheelie bin which was lying on its side in her dad's garden and as she looked closer she could her that dad was lying by the side of it at the top of his path.

He was not moving so she immediately rang 999 and explained that 'her neighbour' had appeared to have had an altercation with a wheelie bin and was in need of urgent medical attention.

She could hardly have said that she knew this because she had seen it in her mirror.

Morgan willed Tabby to go and meow outside the neighbour's house to bring her out to help her dad. Tabby did as he was bidden but nobody would seem to be in.

The front of the mirror was now covered in hordes of unsettled robins which had doubtless appeared there because of her mother's concern for her husband.

It was hard to see Tabby through the throng of upset birds.

She had to get there now, but the only way was to close her eyes and hope that her dad could see her as she could see him and that was assuming he was still alive.

Morgan lay on the settee with Mally by her side and concentrated hard on being beside her dad. Tears were falling freely down her cheeks now and she felt helpless regarding how to help somebody she loved so much.

As she opened her eyes she looked down onto her dad and his aging blue eyes were opening and closing as he was drifting in and out of consciousness. He was alive though and help was on the way. He caught her gaze as she looked into his eyes with tears still falling, "Nice to see you Morgan, how's the cat?" and then he drifted off again. As Morgan looked down she saw his legs were positioned at an awkward angle, but she didn't want to touch anything for fear of causing more damage. He opened his eyes again and said, "Thanks for coming. The horses are playing with the cats look," and then he was out of it again momentarily. Tabby arrived at the scene and put a gentle paw on her dad's arm after leading Caroline, the rather rotund neighbour, to the reason for all the meowing. An ambulance pulled up and her dad was tended by two paramedics before being put onto a stretcher and taken into the back of the ambulance. As he came around again he looked back straight into Morgan's eyes and said, "Wait, can my daughter come in the ambulance with me?" The two men looked where he was looking but could see nobody there. Morgan walked over and took his hand while invisible to all but Tabby and her dad and said she would always be with him and to look after himself. With some effort he squeezed her hand and muttered quietly, "I know love, I'm always with you too. Love you." And with that his eyes closed. The ambulance doors closed on him and the ambulance sped into the distance with its lights flashing and siren blaring.

Morgan watched as it vanished out of sight and then watched as Caroline also vanished back into her home and then she sat down on the lawn with a very concerned looking Tabby and gave the cat a big hug and a stroke. That created a faint purring, but she knew that the cat was as afraid for her dad as she was, "Don't worry Tabby pal, he'll be back home in no time honest."

Morgan slowly opened her eyes and wiped away the tears. Mally was nuzzled up to her neck purring supportively so she lay there on the settee cuddling him and stroking him for a long time. She then got up and poured herself an excessively large glass of wine while waiting for the call from the hospital which she knew was coming.

She would ring Caroline and ask her to look after Tabby until her dad got back home, but right now all she could do was wait on the phone call from the hospital to tell her what had happened to her dad and how he was.

The phone call she had been both hoping for and dreading came about an hour later after she had finished yet another glass of wine. Her dad had broken his hip and had a heart attack and as yet the hospital did not know in which order.

He was alive though and would be monitored before being operated on.

Morgan could only hope and wish for him now from this distance.

Unfortunately, Morgan hadn't seen what was yet to come. During constant calls between herself and the hospital staff as well as with her dad who by now was allegedly recovering but was undoubtedly drugged up to the eyeballs, she assumed that the hospital team would make him better and send him on his way back home to Tabby.

She looked in the mirror and saw that Caroline was standing in the doorway of her dad's home and Tabby was sauntering in for breakfast. She was pleased the cat was being looked after but wished it would be by her old dad again in the near future.

Tabby looked back briefly and directly into Morgan's eyes. She winked at Tabby and the cat meowed straight back at her affectionately.

This was two weeks in and while her dad was making a physical recovery from his broken hip his mental health was deteriorating from what she thought were the numerous drugs he was taking. He also knew something was very wrong and that he had no memory of recent events and even struggled to remember Mally's name and where his own home was. At times it was as though he had regressed and was reliving his younger years and her happy childhood years all over again.

She kept asking the nurses when he would be allowed home as she thought he would understand his own position in life much more easily when he was safely back at home with Tabby and his daily routine reinstated, but nobody would give her a definitive answer.

A month from his admission to hospital a meeting was set up to decide his fate. Morgan had not seen this coming at all, she assumed the hospital would fix her dad and send him back to Tabby, after all they needed their bed back after this long surely if the press was to be believed.

By now her dad couldn't even understand the concept of what the meeting was about, let alone participate in it and this was a man that a month ago was toddling around Cornwall with his pockets full of cat biscuits ready to give a treat to and happily have a chat and a fuss with any cat he came across.

She had spoken to him that morning and he had slurred and forgotten words as he tried to answer Morgan's bland and basic questions. The dad she knew and loved was there somewhere inside and she knew he loved her and hoped he understood how much she loved him, but even some simple words seemed to have no decipherable meaning to him now. He was in the worst place possible.

He was as physically fit as an old man could be and sometimes Morgan picked up on splashes of the intelligent, kind and witty man he had always been, but while his body had recovered well his mind had all but gone and she wondered if in times of clarity he understood the position which he was now in, she sincerely hoped he didn't.

Two doctors had assessed him independently of each other and because they both said he had no capacity to decide the risks that lay ahead of him should he be released back to his quiet existence, and the dangers that reading his newspaper in the conservatory with Tabby sitting by his side might bring, a group of people who had known him for less than a month would be forced to decide if and when he would be free again.

There was a doctor, two social workers, two nurses, and a physiotherapist at the meeting and Morgan took part by way of a conference call so that she could hear everyone in the room and they could hear her.

The doctor and the nurses outlined his medical condition and pondered whether, in their in depth knowledge of knowing him for a month, a man infinitely more intelligent than most, they thought he could work out how to do his own laundry without a washing machine and feed himself; the doctor suggested that even when he was brought in he had been deluded that his daughter had been by his side and wondered if a form of dementia was a possible cause.

Morgan had to bite her tongue on that one, but on whether or not he should be allowed home she was very vocal indeed.

The nice thing with being part of a conference call was that periodically she would hug Mally who was sitting next to her supportively and sometimes she would be looking up at the mirror in which Tabby was looking down at her sitting on the hall floor with the phone in her hand talking into fresh air but somehow the cat knew all future living, feeding and cuddling arrangements depended on the outcome.

Tabby was surrounded by vast amounts of robins which were all looking down attentively so as to see how this looked to be progressing. Morgan knew they were listening in on her mother's behalf and clocking progress.

Interesting view on priorities thought Morgan, bringing her attention back to the meeting in which she was endeavouring to articulate the best thing they could do with her dad would be to let him go back home to his home and his cat.

"Food, drink, shelter, washing machine as priorities," she said out loud. "Must be a Cornish thing."

The robins and Tabby shook their heads from side to side willing her to make a more logical argument for her dad getting parole.

"The body can often overrule the mind," said Dr Ganner in a supercilious tone, as if he had been waiting for this cue for a long time in answer to Morgan's question regarding whether or not her dad's fate could be decided by his own decisions and bidding.

"Even if he has decided his time is up, his body is an incredibly technical and well-designed thing, with the facility to right itself where possible and that will take a lot of overriding."

Morgan gritted her teeth while trying to make an articulate case for her dad to go home while all the others attending the meeting kept describing a frail old man who she did not know that was incapable of making the simple choice to go home.

The only option for now was to accept that he went into a care home with a further review and similar meeting taking place in a months' time. It was agreed that the social worker would let him know the outcome of the meeting.

Morgan was furious as it would appear were the robins looking down from the mirror, but something rather curious was happening in the background of the mirror. Tabby had run to the cottage at the back of the mirror where her dad was bending down to stroke him and a huge amount of snowdrops had suddenly appeared in the garden. Her mother absolutely adored snowdrops.

To the right of the scene was a lovely shiny red sports car which Morgan guessed was a vintage Morgan car and she watched as he picked Tabby up with a big smile on his face and plonked the cat in the passenger seat where Tabby seemed utterly contented. He then wandered casually around to the driver's side, got in and started the engine. As he drove onto the road outside his home he looked back straight at Morgan with a big grin on his face and his eyes were peering lovingly out at her with their spark restored. He waved fondly at her and he and Tabby drove off happily together.

The robins were now calm and an image of her mother was now in the background of the mirror. She looked glamourous and calm with a huge smile on her face as the Morgan pulled up before her, and her husband and his cat got out. She ran over to him and flung her arms around him and the two were locked in a loving embrace for some time. Morgan was happy for them but felt slightly embarrassed about intruding on their private reunion.

Just then the phone rang and a severe sounding nurse on the ward her dad was in said to brace herself as she had some very bad news for her.

Morgan looked up at the mirror to see both of her parents looking back at her with big smiles on their faces and a contented cat with a wagging tail sat to their right.

"He escaped. He got out," said Morgan now with a big smile on her own face. No further words were really necessary.

"I'm so sorry to have to tell you that your father died around twenty minutes ago."

Morgan waved at her parents and they waved back and her dad winked at her.

"He will be much happier now," said Morgan and she put the phone down.

She was calm and happy now as she switched on the telly to see a single pink carnation floating across the image of two hedgehogs in the background.

She looked at the coffee table and a note had appeared on it in her dad's distinct tiny and spidery writing. It read: Dangerous things wheelie bins Morgan love! Don't worry about me I'm off to have some fun – Look after yourself and thanks for the visit. I'm always with you and so is your mum. If I'm really unlucky she'll be able to nag me again now, but at least I bet she won't nag me to put the bin out like she always used to. Much Love Dad XXXXX

She was snivelling as she looked down to see Tabby sitting by her toes looking up at her. She took a note out from underneath his collar which she unravelled to reveal another note from her dad. This time she had to wipe away the tears as she read 'Please look after Tabby. That's my very good friend you've got there and we've seen more than you know together. Thanks love, Dad XXXXX'

As she looked down and gave Tabby a stroke Mally walked up and they gave each other a nuzzle into each other's necks and Tabby proceeded to wash Mally's ears.

Morgan did not know how this was remotely possible but she was so glad that it was. "Thanks Dad, I'll look after Tabby I promise and good luck with Mum. Love you," she said aloud and she blew them both a kiss, knowing they could hear if not see her.

She looked back at the telly to see the screen was full of a mass of beautiful snowdrops and just the two robins singing contentedly together in the foreground at the bottom right hand corner. It was an idyllic picture and the two birds were singing in harmony together perfectly. Did that one on the right just wink at her?

Chapter Sixteen

The Spencers at War

Two Jehovah's Witnesses were contemplating knocking on a door in Lavender Crescent, but decided to beat a hasty retreat from number 13 when they heard the inhabitants having a blazing row with each other.

Roy's day had got off to rather a good start and he had got into the routine of having breakfast and leaving the house to the extent that it had become a routine, and he had forgotten that he was deceiving his wife.

Over the morning coffee and orange juice while looking casually at the racing section of his Daily Mirror he had noticed that Stately Pride was running at Kempton at 2.20pm that afternoon, and as it was over a longer distance than he had run before and therefore an unknown quantity he was likely to go off at a decent price. It was just a shame that Newsboy had tipped the horse and made him his nap, which could decrease his potential level of profit.

Titania and Amber were both trying to sit on their dad's knee so he had no choice but to put the paper back on the coffee table and give his kids his undivided attention for a few minutes. He ruffled their hair and tickled them both and then gently plonked them back on the kitchen floor so that he could give Snowbell a farewell stroke and waggle of his ears. The dog looked up at him rather too knowingly.

Roy would have a toddle over to the bookies later and hoped to see his new friend Ted there and get his advice. The bookies was a nice place to spend time since the miserable woman had left and Jeanie had taken her place, although there were some rumours going around that Tracy the previous cashier had left because she feared the place was about to be sold off. There would always be chatter in that sort of establishment though.

Roy had given his wife a peck on the cheek and left early that morning, starting the day with a walk around the back streets and a coffee in a cheap café he had found near Brick Lane. He had become comfortable and relaxed in his new lifestyle, the only thing missing from it was gainful employment and the cash that came from that.

Maxine was glad to see the back of him. She knew he wasn't telling her something and she didn't like being lied to, although strictly speaking Roy wasn't lying, he was saying nothing, which was probably worse.

Maxine was getting her studio in the spare room ready for Sandy and Lynda to come over to have their nails done later and she put out her most luxurious and colourful enamels and gels ready for them.

After a couple of rounds of toast and a walk to drop the kids off at their friend's house with Snowbell in tow for the walk she was back at home in ample time for their appointment and Snowbell had gone straight to his bed for a snooze leaving them to have a proper girlie time together.

Maxine was quite excited when the doorbell rang and welcomed her friends and clients who had arrived together into her home and gestured for them to go into the studio.

Sandy handed her a bottle of chardonnay and although it was early she popped into the kitchen to open it and then returned to the plush studio with three glasses of the wine on a tray as well as a bowl of salted peanuts to absorb some of the alcohol, which was her logic anyway.

It was lovely to see her friends happy while gossiping together in her home, but she was sure that when she had entered the room they had changed the subject and were almost looking at her sympathetically.

Maxine introduced her new shades and gel finish varnishes to Sandy and Lynda and after much thought and a long decision making process Sandy decided on Candy Ice mails while Lynda plumped for Red Passion.

The wine was gone in no time so Lynda handed her the bottle she had brought with her. This time Maxine fetched some stuffed olives from the kitchen to stop them all getting too tipsy. Who was she kidding?

Again when she re-entered the room the subject would appear to have abruptly changed and feeling somewhat braver due to her alcohol consumption Maxine casually asked why they had changed the subject twice now in what she hoped was a neutral tone while continuing to make their nails look fabulous.

After a couple of firm denials Sandy cleared her throat before saying cautiously that she had been seeing Roy wandering around a lot lately when she would have expected him to be at work.

Lynda nodded and thought for a moment before saying, "He was walking into a pub when I was driving past the other day and it wasn't even lunchtime."

Lynda looked across at a photo of Roy and Maxine on the wall opposite the studio as she confirmed, "Yes, that was definitely him and you did say he worked at a bank full time, didn't you?"

Maxine's mental state was not improved by the alcohol on top of seeming to have her own fears confirmed so she fetched yet another bottle of wine from the kitchen hoping her friends wouldn't notice it was much cheaper than the ones they had bought, and now Sandy and Lynda were just waiting for the varnish on their nails to dry before Maxine applied the top coat to seal them. Maxine wondered aloud if Roy was taking time off work to conduct an affair behind her back.

As she drank more wine she didn't notice the gleeful expressions on her friends faces, they were enjoying the drama they had created and were loving giving out their sage advice. "Why don't you call him at work and see if he's there today?" asked Sandy, who was loving the position of Agony Aunt which she had just promoted herself to. "You're better off knowing what's going on."

The wine had run out and Sandy and Lynda could both see that Maxine was upset although obviously that was nothing to do with them. They paid for their nails and gave Maxine a generous tip and then took their false smiles and Candy Ice and Red Passion nails back out of the house to continue their gossip elsewhere.

Even in Maxine's befuddled and tipsy state she knew these girls were not the proper friends she so craved, but they were at least people who pretended to be.

Maxine took herself into the kitchen and made herself an extremely strong black coffee while making a fuss of Snowbell and asking the dog what she should do.

The seed had been firmly planted now and after finishing her coffee while sobering up slightly, but still festering she decided to phone the bank.

In her best telephone voice, she asked to speak to Mr Spencer and the efficient sounding woman whose voice she didn't recognise on the other end of the line said that he was not available. "When are you expecting him back?" asked Maxine, trying to sound casual.

There was a slight delay before the woman answered "Mr Spencer no longer works here, can anybody else help you?" Maxine was shell-shocked and just managed to mumble, "no thanks," before putting the receiver down and staring at the wall opposite for long moments before getting up and making a fuss of the dog. Snowbell gave her one of his special looks and placed a paw gently on her hand before giving it a lick for good measure. He knew she needed his support.

Maxine made another cup of strong black coffee as she was determined to be something like sober for when he arrived home and she would need to confront him, if not kill him.

He must have been missing work to meet a woman, but who? Maxine racked her brains but couldn't think of any obvious candidates. Perhaps it was someone from the bank. It could even be the woman she had just been talking to. He must be having romantic dates during office hours, probably having great fun and laughing with someone better looking and much nicer than she was.

The tears started to well in her eyes. She did love Roy and they had seen a lot together, but whatever the explanation was he had undoubtedly lied to her and she wondered for just how long she had been being lied to. She thought about phoning the bank back and asking them but decided it would just make her look like an even more pathetic woman than she felt right now.

The girls would not be being delivered back home until early evening as they were being taken to the zoo with their little friend Ethan.

It was just her and Snowbell now sitting in the kitchen examining the evidence and concocting a list of suspects. What other explanation could there be? She must be pretty special for him to give up his job for her, whoever she was.

Then she thought: how on Earth is he paying for the house and the school fees with no job? Is his fancy woman paying or is it all not being paid for anymore? Would he really see her homeless? What if he just upped and moved in with the woman and left her to manage on her own. Snowbell could sense her upset and fear and nuzzled against her soppily. They were having a cuddle when the front door finally opened and Roy said in a cheery voice "I'm home love. Have you had a good day?"

Maxine didn't move from her chair in the kitchen and when Roy walked in to see her sat there looking crushed with a look of fear in her eyes and tears rolling involuntarily down her cheeks, he knew that his time was up and somehow he had been found out.

After a long pause Maxine set him in her Medusa-like gaze and said, "I phoned the bank earlier. They say you no longer work there."

Roy had been dreading this moment, but he knew that it was inevitable it would have happened at some point.

"I've been incredibly stupid," said Roy, honestly, and Maxine immediately fired back loudly,

"Who is she?"

Roy hadn't expected that and tried to embrace his wife who stiffened up and recoiled as he walked towards her.

"It's not a woman love, it's my stupid greed," and Roy held his arms out in a gesture of supplication.

But Maxine had had a long time to fester by now and had decided she must have been betrayed "I don't believe you. Who have you been seeing when you should have been at work?"

Roy was getting more contrite as Maxine was getting even more angry.

Roy finally waved his hands in the air in a gesture of submission and said simply, "I got the sack and was too scared to tell you."

"But you've been leaving here in your suit every morning and you wouldn't have said a word would you unless I hadn't found out. You'd have kept lying to me forever and what about the money?"

It was one long sentence that spilled out at once and showed all of Maxine's hurt and fear in one go.

"It's because I love you that I didn't tell you. I'm spineless, skint, and a liar, but on the plus side I never have and never will go off with another woman, promise."

Maxine laughed despite the awful situation, but it was brief and soon to be replaced by more tears and when she had stopped accusing him of things she used the silent treatment against him almost as a threat.

She looked like a wounded puppy and Roy wanted to take her in his arms and apologise over and over again but touching her didn't appear to be on the cards right now. She glowered at him before saying, "How is this house being paid for if you aren't working. Are we going to end up homeless?"

Roy had no answer but thought aloud that his best option might be to start a business of some sort, after all he was nigh on unemployable and he would need to do something soon to keep everything together.

"I'll go into business somehow love. Don't worry, you and the kids are my world." Snowbell yawned from the dog bed opposite, "And the dog."

A faint smile emerged on Maxine's face, but she was still gutted about being lied to and alternating between loving and hating the man she had married.

Roy was just glad that things were now out in the open. He even ventured to share a couple of his new experiences with his wife.

"It's not all bad love; I've made a new friend while I've been killing time and between us we seem to be quite good at backing horses."

Maxine's scowl and incredulous look were not what he was banking on.

"Seriously! You've got a new mate. Oh, I'm so pleased for you, and you've been gambling when there's only me bringing any money into this house."

Retreating to the corner of the kitchen Roy realised his mistake, he was also keeping half an eye on the clock as the kids would be home soon and he didn't want them to have to walk into a war zone.

"It was a 20-1 winner earlier today, Stately Pride at Kempton. I could even nip out and get us a nice bottle of wine with my winnings."

Maxine had had quite enough wine for one day as well as enough lies and pretend friends.

"Didn't you say your grandad was a bookie once? If you're any good at this why not get a job at a bookies yourself, your good with numbers?"

"Well my new friend Ted pointed me in the right direction with that one actually, but yes I could be good at working out the risks and I certainly enjoy watching the horses run," said Roy while musing about his latest career path. It was certainly a better career path than he had early this morning when nothing further than today seemed to exist and he was a trained bean counter after all.

"Margaret Poulter the Tory would stop trying to get me to stand for election if you did that you know, she wants to close betting offices and for the council to have more powers to stop more premises being granted licences."

Roy ventured close enough to hold his wife's hand, "Every cloud…She's an overbearing woman at best. Did you really want to stand for election?"

Maxine didn't and couldn't be bothered with all the canvassing it would entail, but she still felt that her husband should be backing her in a vocation she didn't even want.

"You're not using my inheritance money or any money from my business in your hair brained plan. I'm not watching money I have worked for disappearing on the back of a horse!"

Roy didn't want a bean off her and would gladly help her with her business if he could, but he had no cash and was certainly not a nail technician.

"I'm glad your business is going well. I'm really proud of you," and Roy meant what he said quite sincerely.

"I'll find a way of getting back on my feet. After all, I've got a beautiful wife and two gorgeous girls to look after. Trust me."

In fact, Maxine did trust him and knew he was sincere, unlike the people she had clung to as friends lately. She had thought she was close to losing him and had only just realised how lost she would feel if he ever left her.

The front door flung open and two very over-excited little girls ran in to their home and bounded into the kitchen with Ethan's very fraught looking mother in tow behind them.

"Thanks for taking them today Mrs Sivyer," said Maxine. "It looks like they've had a great time."

Mrs Sivyer agreed and declined coffee in the now very noisy kitchen, instead deciding to beat a retreat to the relative quiet of her home with just one over excited boy and her extremely quiet husband.

Maxine showed her out through the front door and waved her off thanking her again for taking the kids out for the day.

As Maxine stood at the doorway to the kitchen she heard the girls excitedly telling their dad about all of the animals they had met at the zoo that day.

Roy was playing the clown with them and doing elephant and lion impressions as well as jumping up and down and pretending to be a monkey at one point.

It was as though a weight had been lifted from his mind and it was great to watch them all laughing together. Even Snowbell was getting in on the act by walking around their legs and brushing up to them all in turn for a stroke.

Roy was actually rather good at doing impressions of zoo animals Maxine thought.

"You know if you make a success of whatever you do next the first thing I'll expect you to do is get down to Hamleys and buy us all some of those lovely plush zoo animals they always have in the window."

Roy took the words to mean that a truce had definitely been called and he walked up to his wife and gave her a hug which she reciprocated. They stood there in their embrace for long moments with neither wanting to let the other go and a slightly jealous dog was weaving around their legs vying for their attention, but right now Mr and Mrs Spencer only had eyes for each other.

It was a lovely seen broken only when Amber squealed and fell off a kitchen chair landing on her elbow on the kitchen floor and shouting loudly, "She pushed me, that was my not funny bone too."

Her proud parents laughed and Snowbell went to see if there was anybody in the mirror to show that home life in Lavender Crescent had taken a distinct turn for the better. Family life and keeping it together was very important to Snowbell.

Chapter Seventeen

A Busy Mirror and a Sleeping Cat

Tabby and Mally were getting on like a house on fire, so long as Tabby remembered that Mally was at the top of the food chain in his own house. They were sitting on the settee watching the telly which was rather more interesting than usual due to all of the activity taking place in the foreground of the picture.

The lavender was blowing gently to and fro in a gentle breeze and a very happy looking teddy-bear like white dog was gazing out at them with a twinkle in his dark soulful eyes. Mally pondered briefly whether to get up and show him who was boss around here but decided that he was far too comfy.

Morgan sat beside the cats and stroked both of their heads while acknowledging the now very happy looking Samoyed on the screen. "I'm glad you're happier now," said Morgan out loud, and the dog bowed his head slightly at the words.

The Snow Dust washing powder advert was being broadcast in the background with the beautiful but unhinged looking Elouise Fernandez visible with her near manic eyes glaring out at them, but neither she nor the cats could bring themselves to be remotely scared as they were all focusing on the lovely Snowbell in the foreground.

Somehow though, Morgan knew her involvement with the family from Lavender Crescent was not yet over.

Tabby was half asleep but had now opened his eyes to look at the screen without changing position. A cheerful looking robin appeared in the bottom right corner of the screen and sang an upbeat little tune before leaning forward and looking directly at Tabby while giving the cat a wink.

Tabby half yawned and half meowed back at the robin before looking straight at it and winking back at it. The cat and the robin exchanged loving looks for a moment before another rather flustered looking robin landed by its side and twittered at it with some urgency before looking out of the screen and giving a pretty little chorus of verse before pushing the other robin out of sight as it was shoved along beyond the right of the telly screen and was gone from view.

Morgan smiled at the sight and said merrily under her breath, "Henpecked as always Dad, or should that now be robinpecked?"

She gave the cats another stroke and then returned to her mirror in the hall which was looking particularly lively today.

First a single pink carnation glided gently towards her while an image of Boris the cat sat in the background looking his contented happy ginger self with his big green eyes gazing happily out to her. He was obviously happy enough as he faded out of sight and the image of the carnation faded with him.

An image of her mother's friend Fiona then appeared and she was wearing a sumptuous purple velvet gown with a hood which almost covered her face. She was standing in front of an image of a beautiful chestnut racehorse which was somehow seeming to be a feature in the lives of two of the men she had been watching, sometimes curiously and at other times whether she wanted to or not.

Fiona being there meant that she had to give the horse, or whatever its connection was, some serious thought as it was doubtless a guide to something or maybe even an omen.

She decided it was time for a coffee break and went to the kitchen to put the kettle on. As she walked past the telly there was a clear still image of the bookies in Brick Lane and across the bottom of the screen 'For Sale telephone 01207 565282 Love' was scrawled in her dad's familiar handwriting. She picked a pad and a pen up from the coffee table and immediately wrote down the number under the title 'Bookies in London – Ted and Roy?'

Even as she wrote their names she knew she had not planned to, but that bookies would appear to be a solution for both men and she would phone the number later to see how she could help and how much the shop was for sale for as it evidently was if her Dad had told her so. She pondered at just how bizarre that was as she made herself a large mug of coffee and sat down with her furry friends to ponder events.

If she could work out what to do for the best maybe both men would trundle off out of her thoughts and her mirror.

As she watched the telly again she saw a pink carnation gently floating across the screen with two hedgehogs watching it gracefully go over the tops of their heads and she wondered if James Gazi often spared her a thought as she did him. She hoped their paths would cross again in the not too distant future and she would like to see Boris again too.

Morgan pondered taking herself to the cinema, but as it was a school holiday she decided the battle wouldn't be worth it. It was such a shame they admitted so many children in to watch kids films. She would like to watch the latest Marvel film, but not surrounded by so many small people.

She would do the next best thing on a day off and munch her way through a large bag of Butterkist popcorn while snuggling up to the cats on the settee and working out a solution for all of these people that kept interrupting her natural slovenliness.

And anyway, she couldn't take her cats to the cinema with her so this was much nicer in some ways.

From a selfish point of view, she had to sort out what it was that was required of her so that she could watch telly uninterrupted and use the mirror in her hall to put her hair and make-up straight without having to compete with dogs, fat people and robins.

She ploughed through her popcorn and eventually got up and phoned the number her dad had given her about the bookies. Making out she was a potential buyer she asked about the shops turnover and profits as well as why it was being put on the market.

It would appear to be a reasonable business and was being sold as a going concern as the current owner was wishing to retire overseas. The asking price was sixty grand.

All she had to do now was bring the interested parties together with money she didn't know they had.

As she put the phone down and looked into the mirror Tom and Jerry, the whippets, were looking back at her with bright eyes and shiny coats looking happy in their new home. Ted Clarke was looking even more cheerful sitting on his sofa in the background as he watched over the dogs adoringly.

She looked up at the dogs and said quietly to them "We need to get your new master a job with a purpose, any idea about how to help me do that boys?"

It didn't look like she was going to get an answer until she noticed an open ornate flowery biscuit tin containing a pile of photographs on the coffee table sitting next to a few more photos and the last will and testament of Richard Hart and she guessed that Ted had been taking a trip down memory lane. She wondered if Richard had left Ted well provided for in the will and if he had spent whatever had been there or would he be willing to invest it in a bookies. Sooner or later a conversation would have to take place as she couldn't guess all the answers by looking into a mirror.

It was lovely to see the dogs so relaxed and comfortable in their new home and at least she had some sort of very vague plan forming.

Maybe she could get Roy Spencer and Jeanie to become partners, but hey, this was none of her business really and anyway how could they all get together to discuss this even if it was an option?

It was her day off she told herself as she settled on the settee with Mally and Tabby to watch a film. As least as it was on BBC1 there would be no commercial breaks, meaning she was safe from that scary Elouise and her laundry products.

It was the lovely old black and white film Casablanca. Colourful characters are plentiful in World War II Casablanca, in a waiting room for those trying to escape war-torn Europe. Rick Blaine is a cynical but good-hearted American whose café is the gathering place for everyone from the French police, to the black market, and to the Nazis. When his love interest, Ilsa appears with her Resistance leader husband, Victor, Rick is pulled into both a love triangle and a gripping web of political intrigue. Ilsa and Victor need to escape from Casablanca, and Rick may be the only one who can help them and Morgan so loved the gentle momentum, the romance and drama and was slightly perturbed when a red ford transit van parked up in the middle of the TV screen.

The sedate and elegant film was replaced with two men in tartan shirts and jeans getting out of the transit, lowering the tail gate and putting a plank between the road and the van for them to walk up and down, this was followed by the two workmen bringing two wooden fencing panels out of the truck and laying them onto her next door neighbour's front garden. Morgan did not want to watch any of this particularly and had been thoroughly engrossed in the gentle film which was now forming the background to this activity.

To top it off, five minutes later a banging and clattering could be heard from next door and this was topped off further by the sound of hammering and the two men having a shouty conversation. Morgan presumed they were standing at opposite ends of the garden and yelling at each other.

Unimpressed, Morgan walked up to the window and saw indeed that the red truck was parked outside and the fencing panels were on next door's lawn.

She decided it must be time for a cheese and pickle sandwich as the film was now covered by the truck and even the pleasant soundtrack was drowned out by all the noise.

As she was in the kitchen making her sandwich, a young and very pretty silver tabby padded its way up the plank and into the back of the truck where after a couple of turns it settled into a comfortable ball for a snooze just behind the driver's cab.

Morgan sat back down with her furry chums and took her time eating the sandwich.

After all, with the constant racket and the truck in the middle of the TV screen, still it didn't look like she'd be getting her film back any time soon.

The clattering continued and Morgan really hoped all the men were doing was replacing the two fencing panels as that surely couldn't take too long.

She put the empty plate on the table and wondered why Mally and Tabby were now sat up and staring intently at the back of the transit van. It couldn't be that interesting surely.

The noise from the hammering finally stopped and it appeared that the workmen were tidying up after themselves. She watched the telly as they threw two old and warped fence panels into the back of the truck and then chucked the plank in after them before shutting the tailgate. They then both got into the cab and the driver gave his passenger a cigarette and then lit one himself. They then both sat there puttering smoke and not seeming to do anything else. Morgan wondered why she was being forced to be a witness to this extremely dull and meaningless event that was preventing her from watching her own telly.

Mally stared at the screen still and Morgan looked in precisely the same direction as her boy. Only then did she see the curled up cat which was fast asleep in the back of the van.

She jumped up as the ignition was started in the truck and ran outside flapping her arms about to get the driver's attention before the van drove off.

They weren't looking her way so she ran in front of the bonnet just before the men pulled off.

The driver looked out at her from behind the windscreen with a puzzled expression on his face while his mate looked at him for reassurance as to what he was supposed to do next.

An out of breath Morgan shouted up to them "There's a cat in the back of your truck." That seemed very odd to the men as they hadn't seen a single person but each other from start to finish on this job so how on earth would this woman know that?

Being the patient guy that he was the driver Steve turned off the ignition and wandered to the back of the truck where beyond the old fencing and the plank of wood a very contented and pretty silver tabby was fast asleep and almost appeared to have a smile on its little face.

Steve clapped his hands loudly to wake the cat, whose head shot up at the effrontery of being awakened from what was probably a lovely dream.

It got up, stretched at leisure and sauntered casually to the back of the truck where Steve gently picked it up, stroked its head and plonked the little cat safely on the pavement saying, "Well I never, it's lucky this lady saw you there little one." He was obviously a cat lover. Steve smiled at both Morgan and the cat and then got back into the truck. "No harm done," he said as he beamed a huge toothy smile at them and then drove off waving farewell to them through the rear view mirror.

Morgan waved until they were gone and then bent down to make a fuss of the cat.

The little fella was still clearly underwhelmed at being woken up and looked entirely unappreciative of just having been rescued. To the extent that after giving Morgan a steely look it turned and stuck its tail in the air and wandered off haughtily without even a backward glance never mind any version of a thank you.

Oh well, thought Morgan, you can't please all of the customers. As the cat toddled off to what she supposed was its home a little further down the road she waved it off and said through a smile "here's looking at you kid!"

She went back home and arrived in front of the telly just as the end credits for the film were rolling up the screen. At least the transit was no longer obscuring the picture though. In fact, for a brief time she had a clear view of the news with no robins, cats or trucks at all. It made a pleasant change.

She settled down and watched the soaps and then got rather engrossed in a programme about stream trains, she didn't know that she was remotely interested in steam trains but the programme was narrated by Michael Portillo and he had a lovely soft rolling voice. Morgan thought it was a shame he never got a chance as prime minister, she could have happily listened to his voice repeated on the news every day instead of the insipid and clipped sounding David Cameron.

As she was watching the programme an acrid smell of bleach filled the air and both Mally and Tabby appeared agitated as they sniffed the air. It was most odd as Morgan had not been near any bleach for some time and this was her living room so what was this one all about?

She looked back at the television screen and this time an image of the Mallard was covered by a large image of a pressurised water pistol. Morgan was getting fed up of this.

She picked the plate up from the coffee table and took it to the kitchen to wash as well as her mug from earlier.

As she placed them on the draining board she was still annoyed and as she watched them she saw both the mug and the plate float gently up until they were hovering just below the ceiling.

Oh great, she was displaying her telekinetic tendencies now because she was annoyed. All she could hope was that the mug and plate would land back down on the draining board as gently as they had risen, but there was no guarantee of that.

She poured herself an excessively large whisky and milk which she took back into the living room to drink. The acute smell was now gone, as was the image of the water pistol and she sat down and again listened to Michael Portello's soft voice as he educated her on the history of the railways.

She had just finished her drink and the programme had just ended when there was an almighty crash coming from the kitchen. Both cats jumped down off the settee and looked around in a panic.

Morgan reassured them with a pat on the head each and realizing the mug and plate had landed far from gracefully on the kitchen floor she grabbed a dustpan and brush and scooped them up before her friends could hurt their paws on the shards of pottery.

That was one of her favourite mugs too, it had 'Crazy cat lady' written across it in purple which she thought was very apt.

As she tidied up she cursed Elouise Fernandez under her breath as in her mind there was absolutely no doubt as to her involvement in the recent taking over of her front room and not only was she an uninvited and unwanted guest but she had now broken one of Morgan's favourite mugs.

She took the cats up to bed with her and lay there for quite some time before sleeping as she was still annoyed with the woman and her intrusion into what should be her quiet home life. The cats were a welcome part of it. That wretched woman was most definitely not.

Chapter Eighteen

Preparing the Facts

Morgan was on holiday from the Chronicle as it was that time in October when she would go on her annual theatre trip and she would not go back to work now until the second week in November, so that she could be with and reassure her furry friends on bonfire night.

It was early in the afternoon and she had taken herself for a gentle stroll by the river. As she looked at the weir with its gushing water and listened to the birdsong against the sound of cascading water she vowed to do this more often. It was so beautiful and tranquil and only a mile from home, but for some reason most of the time she forgot this place existed.

This was just what Morgan needed, some tranquillity to figure out what was going on and what she was going to do about it all.

She would also pop into the tourist information office and collect the coach ticket she had booked for her trip to London on the 29th October on her way home. Her theatre ticket was already packed in her handbag ready for the trip and she did like to have everything organised.

Whilst she was enjoying the view and looking forward to seeing the show she still had no clear plan as to what she was supposed to be doing to help the people that had recently intruded into her life, yet she knew she had to help them or she would not be able to do her hair in the mirror or watch a programme in full on the telly for quite some time.

She gazed into a calm area of water by the river bank and the reflections on the water were similar to the reflections in her mind which she was trying to recount and apply some logic too. It was a little easier at this sedate pace.

As she looked down she noticed a mass of bluebells which were being agitated by a strong breeze, but from her postilion on the bank there was only a still calmness.

She had now come to associate bluebells, as well as agitation, with Elouise Fernandez.

Sure enough, on the surface of the water was an image of Elouise swishing her hair about but this time she had a gentle and relaxed smile on her face. It was a vast improvement and Morgan sensed the woman would be happier in the not too distant future. Not that she cared about her that much.

The image faded to be replaced by a smiley Jeanie from the bookies. Morgan wondered why she was even entering her thoughts, but as she looked into her friendly eyes she could see there was some concern there. She thought about the girl and felt just how much she cared about her new job. Jeanie was positively bubbling with enthusiasm for her job. The rumours about why Tracy left and the possible closure of the bookies were circling around Morgan's head now, just as they were flapping around Jeanie's head in London. That was a nice girl and Morgan genuinely wanted to help her if she could.

As she looked back more closely at her young face she had a feeling Jeanie was going to be lucky in some way soon. She would be just fine.

Roy and Ted walked into the bookies together and she beamed at them. There was an obvious fondness between the three of them and it was nice to see.

A barge was coming through the lock a little further up the river, and the rippling it created in the water prevented Morgan seeing anything other than the glistening and lapping on the top of the river's surface until the boat gently continued its journey out of sight in near silence and at a plodding pace and in no particular hurry.

It was a nice distraction and gave Morgan a chance to think as she watched the barge go out of sight with a lovely Labrador dog with a shiny coat and eyes sitting at the rear of the boat looking back at her.

She looked back at the now undisturbed water and saw a cheerful looking Maxine Spencer pottering about her lovely big house in Lavender Crescent with the beautiful Snowbell plodding along beside her.

As she looked behind them in the water she saw some lavender wafting as though it was dancing in the background and she could even smell its soothing fragrance.

It all seemed moderately simple now. She just needed to get this lot together and to get them to think and talk together about the taking over of the bookies as a collective. That was the easy bit. Morgan was far less convinced about what she was supposed to do about Elouise. There was still a feeling of menace that washed over Morgan when she thought about the woman. She was just not likeable.

She may well turn into a happy and well-rounded individual in the future at some point, but right now there was an imminent threat exuding from her and it was unclear where this would be channelled or indeed released. It was also extremely hard to even want to help her as she exuded so much anger and rage, but if she could get shot of her she would do whatever it was that was needed to see the back of her. Elouise had even upset her Mally and that was never likely to make Morgan want to do anything for her.

The connection between all of these people who didn't necessarily know of each other's existence was that they were all based in London and since that was the destination for Morgan's holibobs she would try to see her show and do something about this lot on the same day.

It was all quiet now on the riverbank with not a soul in sight. Morgan just loved water so she raised her fingers slightly and pointed at a lovely still area on the river about five feet in front of her where she then gently floated to. She stayed hovering about six inches above the surface of the river and loved the sensation of having the water beneath her; she stayed there simply enjoying the peace and gentle birdsong for quite some time.

Two ducks swam past her while quacking a conversation between each other and shortly afterwards a swan landed just to the right of her and looked at her quizzically. The landing had made lovely ripples on the top of the river and she turned to the swan and explained quietly that she was absolutely no threat to it.

The swan seamed to understand this as it tucked its wings in and gently bobbed its way further away from her and eventually she watched as it disappeared into the distance in no particular rush.

She raised her hands and pointed back at the riverbank which was still empty of people and landed back not far from where she had previously been standing. She then walked steadily back into town following the line of the river and appreciating the fauna and flora as she went along. She also followed a line of very large willow trees which dipped their leaves prettily into the water.

The bustle of the town was a contrast to the gentle pace of the river and she just wanted to collect her coach ticket now before returning home to the cats.

The young lady with long blonde hair behind the counter of the tourist information centre was very helpful as she handed her an envelope and explained where the collection and drop off points of the journey were and they bade each other a smiley farewell.

All set now, just the cats to apologise to before and after her trip as she had a feeling it was going to be a very long day for all of them, and she did feel guilty leaving them for so long. She also hated all forms of public transport, much preferring to walk to places, but in this instance it was the only available option. One hundred or so miles would be a very long walk.

Morgan walked along the Warwick Road which led out of town but had a road leading off it which would take her in the direction of home.

There were no cars on the road right now, but about twenty yards ahead by the pedestrian crossing she could see something glinting in the road and as she approached the crossing she became more concerned as she saw both a crumpled black and chrome motorbike and a dented zimmer frame lying as though they had been abandoned in the road itself.

She stopped in her tracks as a car was now driving up the road and looked as though it would hit them so she waved her arms around to attract the driver's attention. She managed that alright as he slowed down and scowled at her muttering something under his breath and shaking his head from side to side.

The car then drove straight up the road without hitting anything at all and yet the bike and Zimmer frame were still there unmoved. Morgan watched as a further three cars made their way along that stretch of road without hitting anything and then as she looked at them still lying there inert, she watched as they faded slowly away until they were out of sight appearing to fade and disappear into the road itself.

As she looked on aghast, a stooped elderly woman, with a stern expression and tightly permed grey hair with a very dated looking dress with a colourful and bold paisley pattern as though it were from the seventies, made her way intently to the side of the road. Realising she was supposed to be preventing something from happening here Morgan asked the woman for directions to a hotel which she knew was just up the road and if she knew where the tourist information office was. It was as though the woman hadn't spoken to another person for some time and she appeared not to want to right now either as she gave clipped and direct answers to both questions without a hint of a smile or any eye contact. She grudgingly did spend enough time engaged in a conversation to possibly save her life though.

As they were standing by the road side a rider on a black and chrome powerful motorbike hurled past them accelerating as he went and appearing not to notice the two women standing by the pedestrian crossing whatsoever.

Morgan thanked the woman for the directions as she clearly did not wish to be detained any longer and watched as she safely crossed the road with some purpose if a little slowly.

She continued home and after opening her front door and greeting the cats who both looked up at her with hungry and expectant eyes she looked in the hall mirror and saw James Gazi looking straight back at her very fondly and with a stunning smile showing his glinting white teeth. He then winked at her as her dad was prone to do and her dad's voice came out from his mouth saying, "Well done love, and look after yourself tomorrow. Safe journey." He, or they, then faded away from her, but Morgan knew that would only be temporarily.

She then watched as the old lady from earlier walked slowly across the length of the mirror while leaning heavily on her frame, there was still no trace of a smile.

Behind her was a local yob called Leon Green who was frequently featured in the Stratford Chronicle for all the wrong reasons. He was a petty thief, a bad burglar who got caught more often than not, and a shoplifter who wasn't particularly good at that either. Ironically his mother was well known in the area as she had been the headmistress at a local primary school for over thirty years before she had retired. Rosamaria Green often featured in the chronicle for her fund-raising and volunteer work for many local charities often with her looking very proud in an accompanying photograph.

Leon was actually a well-educated and intelligent man. He just didn't have a clue what he wanted to do with his life.

Morgan could see what Leon was thinking about from this distance and had no intention of going out again today as she would be leaving the cats alone for so long tomorrow, so she looked straight into his eyes with a powerful intent and immediately saw that he didn't like who he was very much or indeed what he was thinking of doing next.

In her sternest voice, which put the cats on edge, she told him to take his headphones out of his ear and listen to her.

Looking in all directions in a startled manner but seeing nobody around but the old woman he sheepishly pulled the headphones out and looked like a small child waiting to be told what to do next.

Morgan concentrated her eyes on his now scared looking eyes and bellowed, "Don't even think about progressing to mugging. That could be your mother the next time somebody thinks they can make a living from robbing off others. Now either help that woman or leave her alone. Oh, and get a bloody job soon!"

She watched as the man looked around in all directions again and then walked up to the woman and offered her a hand crossing the road.

Morgan laughed out loud as the woman turned to him and bluntly said, "Just because I'm old doesn't mean I want to talk to people," and turned and wandered off on her own slowly but in a very aloof manner.

Leon also raised a wry smile at the comment and since he quite liked her spirit he just walked away. He wasn't really a mugger his crimes, or jobs as he preferred to call them, were faceless, but he was wondering now if he had been being watched and spoken to by God and if that was true could he make any money out of letting people know that God was real and in fact female.

Morgan watched on as the two people vanished from her mirror and hoped not to see either of them again. Work over for one day it was definitely feeding time for both her and the cats and she opened the fridge door and gave them chicken slices. They were Mally's favourite, and he knew very well that she was making up for what she was about to do next, but they tasted good and certainly didn't last long. Morgan had doubled up on them so that Tabby didn't miss out, but she was pretty confident Mally had eaten a lot more than his share which was doubtless to exert his position within the food chain to the newcomer.

She settled down with her cats on the settee after preparing a meal of cheesy chips for herself which she later washed down with a few whisky and milks. Morgan didn't even switch the telly on as she wanted to make an extra fuss of the cats tonight so that they would know that they were much loved and would not feel abandoned by her extended leave of them tomorrow.

She gave them both a pat on the head and refilled her glass with what would be her last whisky and milk for quite some time.

As she stood by her front window and looked up at the stars twinkling she felt a nervousness and excitement wash over her.

Looking across the road at the area illuminated by the lamppost she saw Boris doing his nightly rounds of his patch.

He stopped in his tracks to give her a look, but the moment was broken by an owl hooting from one of the trees behind him.

Boris looked somewhat less aloof as he quickened his pace surely on his way by home to his dad's protection. She watched as he toddled off homeward bound looking around just the once to check he didn't have an owl for company.

It was definitely time for an early night.

Morgan, Mally and Tabby settled down for a snuggly night's sleep and there was no way they were moving from the bed until the alarm would go off at 5.00am in the morning.

Morgan slept right through until the clattering of the alarm at the unearthly time but woke refreshed as she had just had a lovely dream in which Jeanie from the bookies was riding a beautiful chestnut racehorse in a field of six horses and she and the horse crossed the line and won the race twenty lengths clear of the nearest rival. Morgan was then privy to seeing Jeanie collect her prize which was a silver tray with a scratch card siting on in. The numbers had been scratched off to show that Jeanie had won a prize of twenty thousand pounds. The girl was ecstatic and although dressed as a jockey she burst into a faultless performance of singing 'Don't cry for me Argentina' to the race day crowd before putting the scratch card at the back of her beige leather handbag and walking back up to the winning horse and giving it an appreciative cuddle.

Then the clattering had begun and Mally and Tabby were up and off the bed due to the racket having disturbed their slumbers.

Morgan put on her fluffiest red mohair jumper, black velvet trousers and her tasselled red suede cowboy boots and proceeded to the kitchen to feed the cats having washed, put some smoky eye make-up on and brushed her hair so that it was a fluffy and big mass.

Mally and Tabby tucked into yet more chicken slices and Morgan drank a huge mug of strong black coffee. She was still upset with Elouise for breaking her best mug but there was no time for that now as she had a coach to catch.

She watched as the cats settled down for a day on the settee together and stroked them while wishing them a fond farewell and then she was off for the short walk to the coach station waving to the cats through the window as she went having first checked for the third time that morning that she had her tickets with her.

A couple of robins sat across the road on a lawn watching Morgan fondly as she walked off into the distance.

Chapter Nineteen

An Eventful Day in London

The journey to London on the coach was somewhat undulating at best and covered a fairly large section of England. At times Morgan felt she was on something of a magical mystery tour, but the driver had the radio on and so she listened to the news. David Cameron was making an announcement in what for him passed as a stern voice, "After discussion with myself Grant Ruffelle has chosen to leave office within this Government as he understands his outmoded views, as have been printed in recent days, have no place in an inclusive and tolerant Government or society."

Morgan was chuffed to hear the news as she thought he was a thoroughly odious man.

The coach finally pulled in to Victoria Coach Station and Morgan disembarked badly needing some fresh air. She walked the short distance to Vauxhall Bridge and admired the vastness of the Thames as she strolled following by its side down the Embankment and up to the Houses of Parliament. An extremely dejected looking Grant Ruffelle was on his own and looking lost as he kept his eyes fixed on the ground while walking through the throngs of crowds in Westminster. She walked past him and felt his anger and confusion, but felt no sympathy for him whatsoever.

It was still only 11.00am in the morning so Morgan decided she had time to bring together a meeting with Ted, Roy and Jeanie before having lunch and getting to the theatre.

She could see as she closed her eyes briefly that Roy and Maxine were currently wandering around Hamleys looked at cuddly toys for their girls. Morgan just hoped they would stay put a little while longer as she hailed a cab and asked the driver to take her to Regents Street.

When she walked into the cuddly toy section of the store she could not see the couple, but as she walked in front of the coffee shop within the store she could hear Maxine laughing as Roy played with a cuddly monkey and giraffe on the opposite side of the table.

Any introduction was likely to be odd so Morgan decided to get herself a cup of coffee and just go for it.

Sitting tentatively down at the table next to theirs Morgan said matter-of-factly, "Mr and Mrs Spencer, I know you don't know me but I've been seeing you for quite some time even though I did not choose to. I think it was Snowbell who wanted me to help you."

Well, they both gazed at her and hadn't called her mad or got up to leave yet so that was a good sign.

"I've seen your face in my mirror before," broached Maxine as a bemused Roy sipped his coffee as a distraction from this random conversation.

"Roy, I've got a telephone number for the agents that are selling GH Ruff Turf Accountants premises and business as a going concern and I've taken the liberty of contacting them. I'd like it if the pair of you, Ted and Jeanie, could meet over lunch in the near future and discuss the matter further."

Roy wondered how this funny looking woman was reading his mind. He would love to run the bookies but what about the cash?

"Actually I was going to meet Ted in the 'Old Nag' for lunch anyway. He gave me a good tip yesterday which led to me being able to buy these for the girls."

He looked down at the giraffe and monkey fondly. Since Morgan seemed to know all about him he presumed correctly that she knew who the girls were which he was referring to and also knew all about Ted.

"How do you fancy meeting Ted over lunch Max? You'll like him and you'll love his dogs."

"Let me finish this coffee and we'll all get a taxi over to Brick Lane together," said Maxine thoughtfully after taking a sip. Roy grinned at her and asked if that was OK with Morgan.

It was odd, but he did feel like this woman had been in his life before today and he knew that she was trying to help them out.

"Let it go," from Frozen seemed to be playing on repeat throughout the store and the coffee shop so it was nice to let that go when they reached the relative quiet of the pavement outside the Oxford Street entrance to Hamleys where Maxine hailed them a taxi to go to Brick Lane.

Morgan was sitting in the back of the cab with Maxine. The glamourous woman gave her a couple of pensive looks before finally asking, "Are you really doing this because of my Snowbell?"

After thinking for a minute Morgan realised she most probably was and answered honestly, "I suppose I am, I much prefer animals to people and your Snowbell is a beautiful dog."

Beaming with the pride of a mother Maxine grinned now. "I think he's special, I much prefer my boy to people too."

Roy leaned around from the front passenger seat "Don't I know it! I worked out my place in the household many years ago." They were all laughing as the cab pulled up outside the 'Old Nag'.

"Tell you what darling, I'll just go and ask Jeanie to shut the bookies and join us for a drink. There's no racing in the next hour so I'll try to persuade her to put a notice in the window and come and join us."

Jeanie was dedicated to her job, but with Roy offering a free lunch and having to admit there were currently no customers in the shop she grudgingly put a sign in the window saying 'Back at 1.00pm," and locked the shop up. In truth she was happy that her company had been requested.

Maxine ordered a bottle of chardonnay for them to share. "Hope that's OK," she said as she handed Morgan a rather large glass.

There was no sign of Ted yet as Roy brought Jeanie into the pub and introduced her to Maxine and Morgan. Morgan noticed the beige leather handbag from her earlier dream was draped over Jeanie's shoulder.

Two silky dogs bounded across to Morgan towing Ted Clarke behind them on their leads. Tom and Jerry made a bee line for her as they obviously remembered her from the mirror. They climbed up her legs and licked her hands and she was happy to give them both a stroke and a cuddle.

"New beer in Ted, 'Winning Post', do you fancy trying one as a thank you for giving me your latest good tip?" Roy shouted across from the bar.

"Great Cheers," said Ted with a big smile back to him.

Jeanie looked thoughtful for a minute, "You know Roy, that could be a good tie in and decent spot of cooperative advertising between the bookies and the pub with 'Winning Post' don't you think?"

Roy winked at her, "Better get you a pint in too then."

They all sat around a large table with Tom and Jerry chewing the tassels on Morgan's boots. As she now had everybody's collective attention she handed the telephone number to ring about the sale of the bookies across to Roy who thanked her appreciatively.

"Tom and Jerry could you pack that in please," Morgan said to the dogs underneath the table and to her surprise they stopped immediately and went to rest their faces on Ted's feet.

Roy addressed his pals around the table, "This young lady has just given me a number to ring regarding the sale of the bookies. It's on the market for sixty grand, what does anybody think?"

Ted thought for a minute and then said, "I could put in twenty grand if we can raise the rest."

Maxine battled with her reserve for a moment before grudgingly saying "I've got twenty thousand that I inherited, but I would expect Roy to work hard and make the business a success."

Roy kissed her and put his arm around her shoulders. "I mean work hard Roy," she reinforced and he kissed her again.

Jeanie took a large swig of her beer and tried to pretend she was invisible which Morgan noticed straight away. She smiled at the girl and suggested she might want to check in the back of her handbag for any winning scratch cards.

Jeanie laughed but did remember buying one the other day and putting it there for safekeeping. She got it out and scratched the numbers off not really expecting to win anything. She then starred at it agog for long moments before quietly declaring, "I've only just gone and won twenty grand!" and draining the rest of her pint in one go.

"That's it then team. We're in!" said Roy. "I'll ring this number later today and put wheels in motion," and he placed the phone number very carefully in his pocket.

"I think we deserve a round of sandwiches to celebrate," and Roy went to the bar and ordered them two large trays of cheese and tomato and cheese and onion sandwiches as well as another round of drinks and a bag of smoky bacon crisps for Tom and Jerry.

They all enjoyed a happy and relaxed lunch together and swapped ideas on what they could do to improve trade at the bookies as well as whether to rename the place. Morgan was just glad this had all come together so well and was grateful for the free lunch and wine. She seemed to have immediately been adopted as their friend and was enjoying watching how well they all got on with each other.

After giving Roy and Maxine her phone number so they could keep in touch and let her know how it all went she slowly walked outside to get a taxi as she was somewhat full from all of the sandwiches. Ted had even given her his contact details and thanked her for coming up with the idea. That was a nice happy ending.

Morgan was going through the lunchtime traffic now in the back of a cab in central London, but she would still make it to the Adelphi in ample time for the matinee.

She was so chuffed at how the meeting had gone at the pub that she even gave the driver a fiver tip.

She entered the lovely theatre and made her way to the auditorium and the entrance to the stalls. The seats were covered in a plush red velvet and as she looked up chandeliers were illuminating the cornices in the ornate ceiling.

The seats were filling up now as she found C3 and sat patiently waiting for the performance to begin. It was only when she noticed who was sitting down next to her that she remembered that she hadn't chosen this seat. She had been guided to be precisely here.

Elouise Fernandez looked stunning and elegant as she sat down without even giving Morgan so much as a glance as she made herself comfortable.

Morgan watched as Elouise put her handbag under her seat and then a carrier bag alongside it and sat back releasing a faint smile as the safety curtain was raised.

A loud speaker announced that the role of Che in this performance would be played by Max Perini and the role of Eva Peron would be played by the understudy Maria Lindsay. There was a faint grown of disappointment from the crowd, but Morgan was quite happy as she knew that understudies often covered weekday matinees and any time this had happened in a production she had previously seen they had been wonderful performers.

As the house lights went down Morgan noticed a faint smell of bleach and looking down for the cause of the smell she realised the carrier bag under Elouise's seat contained a pressurised water pistol full of bleach.

As discreetly as she could she manoeuvred the bag under her own seat with her left foot and firmly placed the heel of her boot on the bag so that it wasn't going anywhere.

As 'Buenos Aires' started up and a young Evita began singing and dancing Elouise looked down for the bag. Seeing Morgan's foot strategically placed to prevent any wrong doing she looked back at the stage but gave the odd glance in Morgan's direction. Catching one of the glances Morgan glared back at the woman and said quietly, "It's not even her you lost out on the role to. Now behave yourself. I am going to enjoy this show and you are going to sit still and not detract from that."

Morgan proceeded to enjoy the first half of the show which included the songs 'Another suitcase in another hall' and 'Goodnight and thank you' before the pounding and upbeat 'A new Argentina' ensured a rousing end to the first act. Everybody clapped and the house lights went up and without even looking at Elouise Morgan grabbed the carrier bag from under her foot and proceeded with a little haste to the ladies' toilets. She was one of only a few people in the room and she swiftly locked herself into a cubicle and discharged the contents of the water pistol down the loo, after all there would be nothing suspicious about a toilet smelling of bleach.

She then checked that Mally and Tabby were alright while brushing her hair in the mirror. They were happily snuggled up together still on the settee and she smiled at them lovingly. Checking nobody was watching she then placed the now empty water pistol and the carrier bag which contained it into the waste paper basket under the sink.

There was just time for a small glass of wine before retaking her seat for the second half of the show.

She sat back down next to Elouise who asked her why she hadn't told the management about what she had planned. "It wasn't for your benefit. I took the easiest option as I've come a long way to see this show and I intend to enjoy it. Anyway, why are you still here? You didn't know I wasn't going to tell anybody."

Elouise looked contrite by now and replied, "Same as you. I love this show and its songs. I would never walk out half way through."

The house lights went down and so the conversation was discontinued as the second half began with a powerful performance of 'Don't cry for me Argentina'. Morgan could see out of the corner of her eye that Elouise was transfixed and seemed to be pinned back in her seat by the gravitas of the song.

'High flying, Adored' and the upbeat 'Rainbow Tour' followed before the symbolic and poignant 'Waltz for Eva and Che' and then the show finally drew to a close with the heart wrenching 'Eva's final broadcast' and the stirring and thought provoking 'Lament'.

Morgan was the first on her feet to applaud a truly magical show with Elouise on her feet and clapping just seconds behind her. Both had tears in their eyes as they looked at each other.

After two curtain calls the cast were gone and the public were slowly filing their way up the aisles and out of the theatre.

Elouise grabbed Morgan's arm and squeezed it gently. "Thank you for not saying anything. I know I'm incredibly stupid and obsessive sometimes."

The last sentence clearly took a lot for Elouise to say as she had stared at the carpet looking embarrassed and ashamed as the words had come out.

At a loss for anything useful to say Morgan smiled what she hoped was a sympathetic smile and checked her watch to see how much time she had to get to Victoria before the coach left. As it turned out she had nearly an hour to get there.

"Please would you allow me to take you for a drink?" asked Elouise in a demure and almost pleading tone.

As Morgan was somewhat intrigued by the woman and as she didn't have anything better to do in the near future Morgan agreed but stipulated it would have to be a venue near Victoria Coach Station.

The two women walked the short distance across London and Morgan actually thought it rather sweet that Elouise held her by the arm as they walked the crowded pavements and Elouise drew numerous admiring glances.

"I wish I got the reception you get when walking down a road," laughed Morgan. "Men keep jeopardising their safety by walking into lampposts just to keep staring at you."

Elouise laughed good-naturedly and lied pleasantly, "You are a very attractive lady."

Morgan knew she paled into obscurity looks-wise compared to this woman, but it was a well-intended compliment none the less.

They reached the aptly named 'Travellers rest' pub just across the road from the coach station and walked the short distance across the pub to the near empty bar.

"How about a bottle of red wine to share?" suggested Elouise.

They took seats at a table in the corner by the lovely mahogany panelled wall and Morgan was surprised at how easily the conversation flowed between them.

Elouise chatted away about the life of Eva Peron and even sang a chorus of 'High flying, Adored' in perfect tune.

"I thought the guy playing Che was very good," said Morgan, "but still not a patch on David Essex."

"He was in the paper this morning," said Elouise after gulping at her wine so that she could get the words out with some urgency "Perini has only gone off with that disgraced politician's wife. Claudia her name is and he is, oh you know…"

"Grant Ruffelle," Morgan interjected. "Yeah, real slick sort, a bit like Perini really," mused Elouise while taking a more graceful sip of her wine.

They continued to chat about big West End musicals including Cats, Starlight Express and Phantom and seemed to like much the same shows and the same songs from them.

It was coming up to time to catch her coach and the wine bottle was now empty so Morgan wished Elouise well for the future. "Your time will come I'm sure," and Elouise got up. "Come on, I'll walk with you to the coach station."

Linking arms as they crossed the road Elouise said "The most I've got to look forward to at the moment is an advert for hairspray." Morgan smiled at her and joked, "Well the next job could be Hairspray the musical."

Elouise escorted Morgan to her coach and waited until it pulled away. She had given Morgan the biggest farewell hug and as the coach pulled away the two women waved at each other until they were each out of sight. Morgan really hoped that Elouise would get her big break soon, she was a charming lady.

Chapter Twenty

A Quiet Day: Any Cats to Save?

It was Halloween as well as being Morgan's birthday. Although she was still on holiday from the Chronicle she had popped in yesterday with cakes for everybody. A solitary pigeon had been standing sentinel outside the front door.

She had gathered together with Rose, Geoffrey and Juliet Moore over a large box of chocolate eclairs and a bottle of pink fizzy plonk and been introduced to the new girl who would be starting off in advertising with a view to becoming a journalist one day. She was thrilled when she turned around to see the very lovely Miranda grinning at her and walking across for a hug if a little surprised, the beautiful girl had dyed her hair a vivid shade of purple.

The day had got even better though when Juliet took her quietly to one side and said that Miranda would be doing Morgan's job as Sammy had gone off to a rival paper giving little notice, so if Morgan wanted the job, when she came back she could be Arts Correspondent. That had to be the best birthday present ever!

Sammy's name was clearly only ever to be spoken in hushed tones henceforth.

After a few too many celebratory drinks she had snuggled up for an evening's uninterrupted telly watching the soaps with Tabby and Mally purring by her side.

She had then enjoyed a lovely serene night's sleep with no odd visions or peculiar thoughts whatsoever.

Morgan looked out of the window on her birthday proper and was a little sad to see the postman walk straight past her house without delivering a single birthday card but then she thought about her promotion at work and was happy again.

She walked across to the mirror in her hall and watched as two robins took the ends of a pink strip of satin ribbon in their beaks and then flew to each of the top corners of the mirror draping the ribbon between then as though it were bunting. The one on the left proceeded to wink at her. "Thanks Mum and Dad," she said back to them.

As the lovely image faded it was replaced by the beautiful furry white face of Snowbell who was sitting happily in his dog bed accompanied by a cuddly Monkey and Giraffe which he would appear to have taken temporary ownership of.

She looked in the background behind him and saw a cheerful looking Roy, Maxine, Ted, and Jeanie having a friendly get together around the kitchen table. In the middle of the table were the details for the sale of the bookies in Brick Lane. Tom and Jerry sat under the table waiting for the crumbs to drop from the croissants they were all eating and were soon scrabbling over them. A scribbled note on the table suggested 'The Lucky Friends Bookmakers' and Morgan did not know whose handwriting it was in, but that seemed to be a fitting name for the bookies. She was glad it was working out for them all and wondered if she would get an invite to the grand opening. It didn't matter too much, she would much rather watch it from home with Tabby and Mally for company anyway.

Her new friends were replaced with a lovely pink carnation followed by a bluebell making their way calmly and elegantly across the mirror. All was well.

As it was her birthday Morgan decided she would take herself out to lunch, but not before she had made a proper fuss of her cats. She might try the new Chinese in town.

After pottering around the house for a while she decided to head into town, but as she opened the front door her plans changed somewhat.

Leaning against the wall outside the door was a huge bunch of the most beautiful pink carnations and a package wrapped in purple wrapping paper with a pink satin ribbon. A small card with a cartoon ginger cat on was attached to the gift.

Morgan looked around but didn't see anyone around so she walked back into her kitchen and placed the flowers into a vase of water and then stood back to admire them appreciatively.

She then took the present into the living room and sat opening it with Mally ready to take the wrapping paper off her hands to play with.

She looked down on the most beautiful framed picture of a pure white stallion rearing with a woman riding him who was wearing a purple velvet robe and had stunning, flowing, long red curly hair. She immediately thought of the image she had seen before of Fiona with the racehorse. The background to this picture was almost psychedelic with every bright colour merging into the next behind the wonderful horse and its mystical rider. Morgan loved it!

As she gazed into it further she saw a clock reflecting in the glass. She checked her watch and was reassured to learn that the clock was precisely seven minutes fast.

She then tentatively opened the little gift card. It read "There is someone who wants to collect you waiting patiently outside, please join me for lunch. James X."

Morgan got up and looked out of the window and then laughed. Boris the cat was sitting on the lawn opposite looking none too pleased at having to wear a big pink ribbon bow around his neck.

Morgan picked up the copy of Death of a Salesman which James Gazi had learnt her, said yet another fond farewell to Mally and Tabby and ventured outside to join Boris. Mally was more than happy playing with the wrapping paper which he had now strewn right across the floor. Tabby was looking on as a grown-up would while watching a recalcitrant child from a superior position.

Boris nonchalantly sauntered across the quiet road to join Morgan and after a stroke or two on his head he set off with her by his side around the corner to his home where two hedgehogs were sitting on the front lawn overseeing proceedings.

James opened the door with a dazzling white smile and wished Morgan a happy birthday.

Boris walked casually into his house and James stoked his head and untied the bow from around his neck. "I think that's served its purpose now pal," he said to a relieved looking cat.

"Come in my dear," and James grandly gestured for Morgan to come in. She was feeling very much like a young girl again in his presence, but smiled and walked into his lovely ornate home.

"I thought we could dine outside as it's such a pleasant day and I know how much you like water," said James as he ushered Morgan through to the back garden where a table and three chairs were set up. Crystal glasses and silver cutlery were perfectly set for two places on a pink silk tablecloth. Morgan wondered who the third chair was for until Boris ambled over and jumped up on to the seat.

"Did you like the picture?" asked James and Morgan replied sincerely that she absolutely loved it. "Good, good. Take a seat with Boris my dear, I'll organise some drinks. I took the liberty of ordering us a Chinese takeaway from the new restaurant in town. I just need to warm it back up, but let's have a drink first shall we?"

James popped back into the house and brought out a bottle of what he said was Muscat Crocant which is a rare and sought after Serbian dessert wine. "Count Rohonczy used to send this rare and exquisite wine Muscat Crocant as a gift to his friends at various royal courts, to famous politicians and men of wealth," said James, again impressing Morgan with his extensive knowledge of all things.

Morgan was just taking a sip when she noticed the two hedgehogs which were in the front garden had just walked under the back gate together and were making their way to the side of James lovely big pond. She took another sip of the wine and watched as the sunlight gleamed on the surface of the water and the trickling waterfall at the far end of the pond. The setting was idyllic.

Morgan then remembered the book which she then returned, even though it had been in her hand up until now, "Thanks for the loan. I've learned a lot. I'm reading up on Churchill now."

James smiled. "If you memorise some of his many quotes to stick in while you're writing reviews you'll do well. He came out with some brilliant one-liners."

That led Morgan to explain about her promotion at work which James didn't look remotely surprised by.

"You're a talented lady. It makes sense for them to use that talent," and he winked at her just as her dad would have.

"Whatever else they may say of me as a soldier, at least nobody can say I have ever failed to display a meet and proper appreciation of the virtues of alcohol. That was one of Churchill's," said James, taking a sip of his own wine.

"Keep Boris company for a bit would you while I get our main courses. Vegetable chow mein with extra mushrooms, hope that's OK"

It was exactly what Morgan would have ordered herself, but by now she had ceased to be concerned about so many coincidences and gave Boris a stroke before walking across to the edge of the pond and looking in at the vibrantly coloured coy carp. A frog sat watching her from beside the waterfall and the two hedgehogs had stationed themselves opposite her looking on, but all was wonderfully calm with the silence only being broken by the sound of the gently trickling water.

James reappeared with two plates of glorious smelling food and they both sat down and tucked in, observed by Boris from his seat.

The chow mein was great and the conversation flowed from Churchill to Boris and his adventures to the playwright Christopher Marlowe and how he died.

James took the plates back into the house and returned with two banana fritters on pink dishes. This was one of Morgan's childhood favourites and she whooshed hers down in no time. James was somewhat more serene and gentlemanly.

"I could lend you a book about the murder of Christopher Marlowe if you like," said James and Morgan nodded and said that would be very interesting, knowing that she would have to see James again to return the book and that was something that she very much wanted indeed.

They had polished off the bottle of wine between them so James gave Morgan a whisky and milk and had fetched himself a calvados, they then toasted 'Happy days' and Morgan said how lovely the lunch, the setting, and the company was. James looked slightly embarrassed as he said that he very much hoped they could do something similar again sometime. Morgan said that was highly likely and smiled as James quoted, "The future is unknowable, but the past should give us hope. That was another one of Churchill's," and he took Morgan's hand and kissed it fondly.

Boris seemed to assent his approval with a single meow and they both made a fuss of him.

After enjoying a stroll around the garden admiring the flowers which James was identifying as they walked Morgan thanked James for the special afternoon and he hugged her. They stayed in that fond cuddle for some time before Morgan said through a big smile, "I'd better show the cats a good mother," and picking the book up which James had lent her. She kissed him gently on the cheek and was escorted to the top of the garden by Boris who she stroked and wished a good evening.

James walked to the top of the garden and said quietly, "If you ever need me I'm only seven minutes away you know."

She set off home and waved until James and Boris disappeared back into their home. She had had a lovely time.

As Morgan let herself into her home she saw shredded purple wrapping paper strewn all around the living room. The two suspects that were inevitably responsible were curled up fast asleep, cuddled together on the settee having no doubt had a fine old party. Morgan just laughed and ruffled the fur on their heads, especially the chief suspect that was Mally.

After rummaging under the kitchen sink Morgan found a hammer and a nail which she banged into the wall of her hall to the left of her mirror waking up her furry friends in the process. She then proceeded to hang her lovely new horsey picture next to the mirror and stood back to admire the image of the horse and the merging colours behind it. Again as she looked into the glass she saw a clock reflected back at her and was pleased to note that it was still seven minutes fast.

Looking to the right of the picture Morgan saw a very gorgeous Elouise Fernandez swishing her shinny hair about with a great big smile on her face. At first she thought this must be Elouise's new hairspray advert being reflected until she remembered that she hadn't switched the telly on.

Upon closer inspection she saw that Elouise was holding a letter in her hand. She was moving animatedly and so it was hard to read at first but Morgan finally deduced that the letter was headed 'Congratulations!' had the words 'New serialised drama' in the middle, and 'Look forward to working with you' at the bottom. Even without reading this based purely on the enormous smile on Elouise's beautiful face which made her look even more stunning, it was clear that she had landed a job which she was more than a little bit happy about. Morgan was absolutely thrilled for her.

Just then there was a knock at the front door. Morgan couldn't see anyone through the small glass crescent window at the top of the door and she noted that it was starting to get dark, but she felt an innocence coming across from the other side of the door and so she opened it.

"Trick or treat!" yelled five grinning small children, one of whom unfortunately had a front tooth missing and so whistled while he was saying the words.

Morgan didn't have any sweets in the house and so opted for a trick instead. The kids were just about to throw what looked like glitter at her when thinking of the vacuuming it would bring about she said, "Woah! How about I do a trick instead?"

The kids nodded and looked on expectantly as Morgan pointed at the ceiling and then back to the floor four times therefore rising and falling and seeming to bob up and down in the air.

"You're cool," declared a little blond girl and, "Mega," decided a mousy haired girl with big brown eyes and then they turned on their heels and were gone in search of sweets from the unsuspecting neighbours.

"Wait until I tell my mum," said the blond girl as they were heading down the road in pursuit of sweets, but Morgan knew very well that she had nothing to worry about as the mother or any other adult simply wouldn't believe a word of it.

Morgan shut the door and chuckled, she rather liked being thought of as cool.

She walked into her kitchen and admired her lovely carnations. The smell of the perfume coming off them was beautiful and it seemed to be interlaced by the scent of both lavender and bluebells now.

Morgan poured herself a whisky and milk and sat down on the settee with Tabby and Mally. She leaned over to where she had put the book about the murder of Christopher Marlowe on the coffee table when she had come in and turned it over to read the blurb. As she did so a little note fell out on to the carpet. Morgan picked it up to read, 'Remember, we are only seven minutes away if you need us. James and Boris X,' and he had even done a little cartoon drawing of Boris the cat.

There was an air of peace and happiness now in her home and after wishing for solitude in her house for some time now she really hoped that she would see how all her new friends were getting on in the future and wished them all well.

Still, she had the new job she had coveted for ages and a charming pair of friends living just around the corner.

More importantly, she still had a few days off to enjoy with Mally and Tabby and it would be nice just to watch the telly without constant interruptions which she couldn't watch the programmers through.

She walked across to the telly and switched it on. She was watching the local news when two robins walked in front of the newscaster and started tweeting something that sounded a bit like somebody gargling while singing 'Happy birthday to you'.

"Thanks mum and dad," she said and the one robin winked before the image faded to be replaced by the weather forecast.

Morgan agreed with the young lady standing in front of the map, the outlook was definitely fine and mild with sunny spells and she might even take herself for a gentle float up and down the river tomorrow since as the nights were drawing in she would be pretty close to invisible in the evening.

Epilogue

All is for the best in the best of all possible worlds
Voltaire.

A small and scraggly, but very furry, black and white cat had been loitering with intent around Morgan's house for the past couple of days much to the consternation of her resident cats Mally and Tabby.

This evening as she was putting the milk bottles out it took its chance and was through the front door before you could say, "I'm moving in, thanks."

Morgan was looking forward to watching the new drama on the telly tonight. It was a two-part thriller, called Risk Assessment: Murder, and an unknown actress, who was very much known to Morgan, was about to make her debut on prime time TV.

"OK Evita, you can stay," said Morgan addressing the small cat she had instantly named that was already sitting very comfortably on the arm of her settee, "just don't meow through this, I'm looking forward to seeing how Elouise Fernandez does."